MAGIC UNDERGROUND

MAGIC UNDERGROUND

THE WITCHES OF PRESSLER STREET™ BOOK SIX

MARTHA CARR

MICHAEL ANDERLE

This book is a work of fiction. All of the characters, organizations, and events portrayed in this novel are either products of the author's imagination or are used fictitiously. Sometimes both.

A Michael Anderle Production

LMBPN Publishing
PMB 196, 2540 South Maryland Pkwy
Las Vegas, NV 89109

First US edition, April 2020
Version 1.02 May 2020
eBook ISBN: 978-1-64202-838-6
Print ISBN: 978-1-64202-839-3

THE MAGIC UNDERGROUND TEAM

To the Early Readers Team
Kathleen Fettig
Michael Robbins
Debi Sateren
Michael Baumann

Special shout out to Grace Snokes, Lynne Stiegler, Judah Raine, Kelly O'Donnell and Stephen Campbell for their general badassery behind the scenes to keep everything running so smoothly.

DEDICATIONS

From Martha

To all those who love to read, and like a good puzzle inside
a good story
To Michael Anderle for his generosity
to all his fellow authors
To Louie and Jackie
And in memory of my big sister,
Dr. Diana Deane Carr
who first taught me about magic, Star Trek,
DC Comics and flaming cherries jubilee

From Michael

To Family, Friends and
Those Who Love
To Read.
May We All Enjoy Grace
To Live The Life We Are
Called.

CHAPTER ONE

"Magic's only been totally off its rocker for...what? A few days, right?" Emily Hadstrom shook her head as she and her older sisters Nickie and Laura climbed the steps from the sidewalk up to their old Victorian-style house at the top of the small hill on Pressler Street. "That fairy acted like another unawakened Peabrain when we dropped him off with that transport bubble. Like he'd never seen magic before."

"Leonidas deserves a little more of a break, Em." Laura spread her arms and shrugged. "The guy had his apothecary raided by the Gorafrex, was kidnapped—with me, by the way—and had no idea what the energy core was for or how in the world the three of us managed to pop the Gorafrex off into a different dimension using nothing but an iron lance and a few potions."

"Hey, don't forget that whole suspended-without-gravity thing." Nickie turned around and pointed at her sisters with a half-smile. "That was like...magic working in reverse."

"Or magic working to reverse the natural laws on this ship. Like gravity and physics." Laura brushed her long dark hair—the same all three Hadstrom witches had inherited from their mom—back over her shoulder. "Not sure which one it would actually be at this point."

"Well, good thing your boyfriend's a physics professor, huh?" Emily elbowed her oldest sister in the ribs and laughed. "Like, how lucky did you get with that one, huh? Whatever questions you can't answer, Laura, turns out Nathan can."

"I don't know if I'd necessarily call that *lucky*, Em. More like compatible."

"What? *Compatible*?" Emily stopped in the middle of the walkway halfway between the top of the stairs and the Hadstrom sisters' front door. "Wow. Talk about a hopeless romantic over here, huh? You sure you can't come up with a better description than that?"

"Maybe I could if I wasn't…" Laura stopped a few feet ahead of her youngest sister and cocked her head.

Nickie looked up from staring at the yard beneath her and studied Laura's frown. "If you weren't what?"

"Wondering what the heck's going on in our house right now."

"What?"

The Hadstrom sisters all looked up at their house, which now flashed from the inside with a multitude of different-colored lights, one right after the other.

"Looks like someone's throwing a rave in our living room," Emily muttered.

"I seriously doubt that Chuck and Nathan would have

anything to do with raves." Nickie cocked her head and shifted her weight onto one leg. "Okay, maybe Chuck. If I went with him. But not Nathan. And they definitely don't have enough firepower between the two of them to be blasting off that kind of magic."

"I seriously hope not. Come on." Laura headed up the walkway again toward their front door, and her sisters followed.

Emily blinked quickly and shook her head. "Wait a minute. You hope they don't have enough magic for that? So…you're hoping that something in our house that we don't know about *does* have enough magic to throw a rave in our living room?"

"No, Em." Laura paused on the cement block of their front porch and held up a hand for her sisters to wait. "I meant that I hope it's not them getting in trouble with magic nobody can control, lately."

"Except for us." With a smirk, Emily folded her arms and raised an eyebrow at her oldest sister. "'Cause we have the Hadstrom-magic jumper cables."

Laura puffed out a sigh and held her open hand toward Nickie. Nickie grasped it, then grabbed Emily's fingers with her other hand until the sister witches formed a chain on their front porch. "Don't try to cast anything until we know what's going on, okay? The last thing we need is for three spells to backfire at the same time because we couldn't decide on where to funnel our focus."

"Got it." Emily nodded.

"Yep."

"Okay. One…two…three." Laura twisted the doorknob

on their front door, which was fortunately still unlocked, and shoved open the door. The flashing, multicolored lights continued inside, now punctuated by high-pitched shrieking every few seconds after a particularly bright flash.

The sisters stepped inside, all connected by their hands, and Emily lashed her foot out behind her to slam the door shut. The source of all the surprised yelling and the out-of-control spellcasting in their living room didn't seem to notice the Hadstrom sisters had come home. Quickly, Laura, Nickie, and Emily rushed across the foyer and into the living room on their left. They stopped right inside the entryway and stared with wide eyes at what none of them had expected to see.

"Wow. Look at that." Emily dropped Nickie's hand and scratched her head. "A Peabrain with broken magic."

Nickie glanced back over her shoulder and hissed, "That's *Dave*."

"I *know*."

And there he was—the owner of Blue Silk Records, Chuck's best friend, and the last human host the Hadstrom sisters had saved from the Gorafrex's possession. Dave's hands were outstretched in front of him, sparks of every color bursting from his fingertips as he tried in vain to aim them away from anything that might be severely damaged from his lack of magical control. Which was probably everything.

A sharp bark and a whine came from the ceiling. The Hadstrom sisters looked up, and all three of their jaws dropped when they saw their immortal bulldog Speed doggy-paddling through the air right below the ceiling, suspended by bubbles of Dave's unhinged magic that apparently had no intention of bringing the family pet back down where he belonged. Nathan had gotten up on the couch and now jumped as high as he could, swiping at Speed's back paws and trying to get hold of the poor animal.

"Wow." Nickie ran her hand through her dark hair. "Em and I leave for a few hours to go rescue Laura from the Gorafrex, and *this* is our big 'Welcome Home,' huh?"

Dave let out a yelp of surprise and whirled toward the sisters. A barrage of brilliantly flashing silver bubbles lighting up the living room like a few dozen disco balls hurtled from the man's outstretched hands. All three Hadstrom sisters ducked, and the magical bubbles soared over their heads to wreak havoc somewhere else in their house.

Nathan stopped jumping on the couch. "You're back!"

"Of course, we're back." Emily gestured to Laura. "And we got her."

"Okay, try this!" Chuck came barreling into the living room from the mudroom in the back, brandishing the sisters' bright-yellow broom. He skidded to a stop when he saw the witches standing right off the foyer and grinned. "You did it."

"And you guys have obviously been busy." Laura glanced up at Speed, who'd now given up on trying to swim through air and had taken up his usual lazy slump on his belly—on top of a bunch of Peabrain bubbles, this time.

Nathan laughed and bent to climb off the couch.

"Woah, woah. Get the dog down first."

"Right." The physics professor nodded at Chuck, who

seemed to have forgotten about the broom in his hand. Chuck blinked, tossed the broom to Nathan, and leapt aside when Dave's stream of nonstop magic sent what now looked like fishbowls full of miniature safari animals flying toward the back of the living room.

"Oh, come on!" Nathan swiped at Speed with the broom, but now the bubbles had taken the dog far enough away that even the lanky professor couldn't reach him with the broom's extra five feet.

"Guys, I have no idea what's going on," Dave muttered. "I thought I'd gotten the hang of this weird magic thing, but now it's—"

He lurched forward and looked like he was about to vomit. What came out of his mouth instead was a string of bright-yellow bubbles.

"Well, it could be worse, right?" Emily shrugged and stepped toward him. "At least your magic's not—"

The first few bubbles falling out of Dave's mouth hit the hardwood floor and burst with a sizzling pop and a flash of bright light. Smoke curled up from a charred dent the size of a penny in the wood, then the next two bubbles burst on the floor the same way.

"At least his magic isn't dangerous?" Nickie eyed her little sister sideways. "Is that what you were gonna say, Em?"

"Pretty much."

"Sorry!" Even Dave's shout was muffled by another string of bright-yellow bubbles, only these moved much faster and seemed to be seeking out new targets. The first few scattered across the wall inside the foyer, peppering the old plaster like a spray of machinegun fire. His hands still flashed with multi-colored sparks. "Help."

"Not the best time for fireworks," Laura muttered.

"Lemme see what I got." With a quick nod, Emily spun on her heels and rushed across the foyer into the dining room, where only hours before, she and Nickie had used the final tracking potion to help them find Laura.

"Hurry, Em." Nickie grabbed Laura's hand and squeezed. "So, like you said, let's get on the same page."

"Right. Probably—"

The witches ducked as the bubbles that had lifted Speed to the ceiling now dropped and whisked the startled bulldog toward them like he was riding a magic carpet. Dave's accidental exploding bubbles followed the poor dog all the way into the dining room.

"Shields." Laura nodded. "Just shields."

The Hadstrom family legacy rings on both sisters' thumbs—silver for Laura and black for Nickie—flashed with their respective colors. A wall of shimmering pearlescent light rose in front of them right before half a dozen sparking, exploding bubbles hit. But, Dave's magic bounced right back off, sending the yellow bubbles whizzing back through the living room in every direction.

Nathan swung the broom at the two bubbles heading toward him. One exploded, but the other headed right for Dave as another string of magic hurtled from the awakened Peabrain's mouth. All of them burst and sparked and squealed. Dave dropped into a crouch, covering his head with his arms, Nathan tumbled backward off the couch, and Chuck dove across the floor onto his belly to avoid the tiny yellow birds that had popped free from a handful of the bubbles.

"Dave," Nickie called. "Try to calm down, okay?"

"Calm down?" The bewildered Peabrain jerked his head up to shoot the witches an incredulous look. "I don't know what's hap—ow!"

He flinched away from the sparks still bursting at his fingertips, and the strong stink of burnt hair filled the living room.

"Dude." Chuck crawled toward his friend as the yellow birds fluttered and dove all around the living room. One of them headed straight for the mantelpiece over the fireplace on the far wall. Its dangerously sharp beak hit the carved wood, and the bird stuck there like a thrown dart. "What if you, like, ask nicely for everything to settle down?"

"Ask *what*?" Dave's eyes widened as even more bubbles streamed from his mouth. This time, though, they were a deep, navy blue and started swirling around him, moving faster by the second.

"I don't know. Magic?"

"That's not really how it works, man." Nathan stood from behind the couch, dusting off his shirt. Two more firecracker bubbles shot toward him.

"Watch it!" Nickie lifted her hand toward the professor. Her black ring flashed, and the yellow bubbles burst in front of Nathan's head, pelting him with tiny marshmallows instead of searing sparks. "What?"

"Thanks." Nathan stared at the marshmallows scattered at his feet. "I guess that works."

Laura pointed at the dark blue bubbles swirling around Dave, wanting to slow them down a little. Her silver ring flashed, and the blue bubbles coalesced together into one massive ball in the center of the living room that now looked like it held a growing thunderstorm.

"What are you doing?" Nickie muttered.

"I don't know!" Laura blinked. "That definitely wasn't what I was going for."

CHAPTER TWO

"Hey, Em!" Laura called across the foyer. "Anytime now with those potions would be great."

"Yeah, yeah. I'm working on it. Just need a—hey!" A thump and loud crash came from the dining room, followed by a chorus of startled squawks, frantic flapping, and Speed's harsh, sharp bark. "Birds now, too? Speed, get off the table!"

The dog thumped onto the floor, rolled, and started chasing after the dart-like yellow birds in the dining room. His nails clicked on the hardwood floors.

"Hey, look." Dave held up his hands, and everyone else in the living room flinched automatically. "No more sparks."

"Great, buddy." Chuck pushed himself up off the floor, sat back, and stared at the still-growing orb of dark blue thunderclouds and silver-streaking lightning that was now twice the size of the coffee table. "Now do something about that storm in a bubble."

"I don't even know what it is." Dave puffed out a sigh and stood. "Maybe if I—"

"No, Dave, don't touch it!" Laura's warning came too late.

The minute Dave's fingertips reached the outside of his unrestrained magic, thunder boomed inside the Hadstrom sisters' living room. The flickering lightning inside the huge bubble crashed through the barrier and lashed out at the wall over the fireplace. It seared a jagged scar in the mantel, freeing the stuck yellow bird, and cut a swath of burning light all the way toward the back of the house.

"Em!" Laura squeezed Nickie's hand even tighter as two more forks of lightning shot out from the giant bubble. She focused everything she had on containing the electric bolts still inside it. Her and Nickie's rings both flashed, and the next lightning strike didn't make it out of the bubble. But the brewing storm inside rumbled, and the contained magic shuddered like it was about to explode.

"Got it. Got it!" Emily darted back across the foyer into the living room, froze when she saw the charred lines of lighting-fried wall, then lifted the finished potion in her hand. "This should work."

"*Should?*" Chuck shouted.

"Didn't have a lot to work with. Just—hey. Speed! What—"

The dog darted under Emily's feet, barking and snapping at the yellow birds flitting around the living room. Emily tripped, lunged forward, and the potion vial flew out of her hand. At the same time, Nickie reached out and clamped her hand around Emily's ankle, lending her sister the backup magical power of all three Hadstrom witches together—the only way any of them got magic to respond even a little to their intentions.

With a shout of surprise, Emily reached out toward the flying vial. Her copper legacy ring flashed on her thumb, and the vial changed directions mid-air to veer toward the storm bubble before disappearing right inside the dark blue thunder clouds. There was a little pop, another electric charge burst through the living room, and the storm bubble shrank into itself. A gush of water splattered across the floor and all over Emily, and then the entire room was silent.

"Ow." Emily grunted and pushed herself up onto her knees, where she'd landed. Another yellow bird darted in front of her, quickly followed by Speed. The dog used Emily's lap as a springboard and jumped high enough to catch the tiny bird's tailfeathers in its teeth. The bird squeaked and disappeared.

"Wow." Dave took a step back from where his misbehaving magic had almost torn the living room apart. His shoes splashed in the puddle of magical rainwater. "Is that…"

"Looks like that's it." Laura released Nickie's hand.

"Hey, guys, I'm so sorry." Dave glanced at his hands with wide eyes. "I don't know what's happening."

"Yeah, most people don't right now." Nickie set a hand on Emily's shoulder. "You okay?"

"Oh, yeah. That's not my first time falling over in time to stop things from getting worse." Emily chuckled and rubbed her chin. "Could've bitten my tongue off, though."

"Not like there's a real reason these days for magic to act out and do exactly what we don't want it to…" Nickie stepped toward Dave and cautiously spread her arms. "But it might help if you can think of anything that maybe set this off."

"Uh... I was trying to go over the list of all the things I've missed in the last few days." Dave scratched his head and scanned the sopping floor. "You know, work stuff. Trying to figure out when happened when I...when that thing..."

A few more sparks burst from the guy's fingertips.

"Watch it." Nathan pointed at him.

"Woah, woah." Nickie cautiously stepped away again.

Emily nodded. "Stress magic. That definitely looks like stress magic."

Laura shot her youngest sister a quick glance and nodded. "You would know."

Chuck quickly stepped across the living room and grabbed his friend by the shoulders. "Dave. Buddy. Look at me."

Dave's head jerked up, and the sparks died out again. "Yeah."

"Everything's okay, man." Chuck nodded slowly and gave the owner of Blue Silk Records a reassuring smile. "All that's over now, yeah? Smooth sailing from here on out."

"Dude, nothing that just happened was smooth."

"But it will be." Emily pushed herself to her feet, wiggling her sore jaw back and forth. "Gotta stay positive, Dave. Try not to think about what happened, okay?"

"Yeah, and maybe give yourself a little more time before you dive back into work." Chuck gave his friend a few quick pats on the back. "Keep things low key."

"Low key. With magic, now." Dave nodded, drew a deep breath, and shrugged. "I can try."

"Yes, you can." Emily pointed at him and grinned. "And now that you got things back under control, I have a little more time to come up with something for you, okay?"

Without waiting for an answer, Emily spun around again, sloshed through the water on the floor, and headed back into the dining room. Her wet sneakers squeaked across the hardwood.

"What's she talking about?"

"Potions," Laura and Nickie said together.

"It's kinda like she was born to make them," Nickie added.

Dave glanced from one Hadstrom sister to the other. "So, she knows what she's doing."

"Yeah, mostly."

The color drained from Dave's face, and Chuck gave his friend's shoulder another little shake to jolt him back to the present. "Hey, trust me. Whatever Emily has planned, it'll work for you. And she knows what she's doing. She started teaching *me*, believe it or not."

"You?" Dave cocked his head.

"Wait, what?" Laura turned to look at Nickie in surprise.

"We did a lot in not much time to find you." Nickie shrugged. "Chuck was really helpful."

"See?" Chuck spread his arms and grinned. "I might be the token human with no magic, but I *can* do useful stuff like help with potions. I think the word *apprentice* might've been mentioned."

"Wow." Laura blinked at him.

"And Nathan was really helpful, too." Nickie pointed at the professor, who'd stopped at the edge of the slowly spreading pool of water. "You should ask him about that later."

"Okay." Emily rejoined them with three different potions vials in her hands. "This is a start, Dave. Kinda precautionary right now, but here's what I have. Blue is for stopping whatever crazy magic bursts out of you that may or may not end up hurting somebody. Like the one I used in here. Pink is to make something scary or painful or potentially dangerous turn into…the opposite of those things. It doesn't take the whole potion, so you have maybe three tries of each."

She handed the vials to Dave, who took them like they might explode right alongside his firework bubbles. "What about this yellow one?"

"Oh. That's, uh…more like tea."

"Tea, Em?"

"Yeah. I already had all the herbs." Emily nodded at Dave. "It'll get you to chill out if nothing else works. And maybe that's the best place to start."

"Cool." The Peabrain stared at the different-colored potions, then tucked them against his chest and nodded at everyone in the living room. "I knew coming here was a good idea. Thanks."

"You're totally welcome." Nickie shot Chuck a questioning glance. He shrugged.

"Now that you're a little more prepared," Laura said, guiding Dave back into the foyer and toward the front door, "you can give yourself a break and take the time to learn how to handle this kind of stuff by yourself."

"I tried..."

"Of course, you did. You don't exactly have it easy, figuring out how to use your magic when magic doesn't even work for people who've been using it their whole lives. But that should be changing soon if we have anything to say about it."

"Okay. If I need help again, though—"

"Try the potions first." Laura opened the door and held it open with a reassuring smile. "And if those don't work, call one of us."

"Yeah, I'll call before I come over next time."

"Or call us first," Nickie added, "and we'll come find *you*. Probably easier for all of us that way."

"Yeah. Makes sense, I guess." Dave nodded and slowly stepped onto the front porch, his eyes wide and a little glassy.

"Remember, Dave," Emily called from near the foyer, "potions need to be taken care of, too. Keep 'em cool and dry, and don't shake 'em too much."

"Got it. Thanks, guys."

"Yeah, no problem." Laura smiled sweetly and slowly closed the door, watching Chuck's friend heading up the walkway toward the steps. "Good luck."

CHAPTER THREE

When she finally shut the door, she made sure to turn the deadbolt this time, then leaned back against it with a sigh.

"Hey, babe?" Nickie called over her shoulder, although she didn't completely look away from Laura.

"Yeah?" Chuck stepped out of the living room to join them in the foyer.

"Did you tell Dave he could come over here if he was having problems with his magic?"

Chuck raised his eyebrows and a finger at the same time. "Definitely not. You saw how much he's been calling me the last few days. Like, every time something even remotely magical happened. I think he put two and two together and figured it was his safest option."

"Well, at least he can still put two and two together with totally unhinged spells like that." Laura drew a deep breath and tilted her head from side to side to stretch her neck. "But we still have a lot going on right now, and it's not ideal to have people showing up out of the blue because they didn't know what else to do."

"By the way, that doesn't apply to you guys." Emily clapped a hand on Nathan's back and pointed at Chuck. "You guys are cool."

"Thanks, Em." Chuck rubbed the back of his neck. "So next time, you want me to turn him away and tell him to figure it out on his own until one of you calls him back?"

Nickie wrinkled her nose. "It sounds kinda harsh when you put it that way..."

"Yes, Chuck." Laura pushed herself away from the door and nodded. "That's the best way to handle something like that. At least until we put magic back together so it's working again. The right way. And we're not supposed to be helping Peabrains figure out their magic in the first place. I mean, even potions might've been a little too much."

"But they sure did make him feel safer." Emily spread her arms. "That's pretty important, especially right now."

"Yeah, Em," Nickie added. "I think we can go ahead and say that Austin—and all of us—are probably a lot safer now. For a little while."

"Woah." Chuck's eyes lit up and he gazed quickly from one Hadstrom sister to the next. "Did you actually do it?"

Nickie chuckled. "We've done a lot in the last little while, babe. Specifics would be nice."

"So, *specifically*, did you guys stop that thing? The Gorafrex? Sorry, I should've asked sooner, but the whole Dave thing... You did, didn't you? You got it back into the prison." Chuck almost skipped toward Nickie and grabbed her shoulders, grinning like he'd won the lottery. "I knew you could do it. That means all this craziness is pretty much over, now."

"Not exactly, Chuck."

When he looked up at Laura, she shook her head. "We *did* capture the Gorafrex—"

"Great!"

"*But* it's not back in the iron prison," Emily added, clasping her hands behind her back. "Not yet."

"Okay..." Chuck frowned. "I don't get it."

Nickie set her hands on her boyfriend's hips and tried to look optimistically convincing. "We ended up sending it into the Clubhouse. Everything else kinda fell apart when the other energy core exploded and the natural laws of physics stopped working for a little."

"*What?*"

"But it's no big deal."

"Right. We'll figure it out." Emily shot the guy two thumbs-up. "We always do."

"Yeah, eventually..."

"Oh, come on, Chuck. That's not the right attitude."

He nodded at Emily and offered all the Hadstrom sisters a half-smile. "I'm glad you're back and you're safe and your living room didn't burn down. I thought it might, for a second."

Nathan cleared his throat, and everyone turned to look at him. He leaned against the entryway into the living room, his arms folded, and gazed intently at Laura. "You guys are completely missing the most important thing right now."

"Uh...we are?" Emily frowned up at him.

"What's that?" Laura stared right back at him with a

light blush rising in her cheeks, although she was slowly starting to smile.

"That your sisters found *you* and got you away from that thing."

Laura swallowed and couldn't even blink. *Why is he looking at me like that?*

"That *is* pretty important," Nickie added. Chuck rubbed her arms a few times, then finally decided to wrap his arm around her instead of clutching her in excitement.

"And we couldn't have done it without your help." Emily playfully jabbed her fist against Nathan's arm. "Oh, Laura, you're not gonna believe what we had to do first. Or how helpful it is to have a Kashgar around when we're trying to figure out some ancient technology underground—"

"Part Kashgar, Em." Nickie wrapped her arms tighter around Chuck and pressed her cheek against his chest. "And I already told Laura she needs to ask Nathan all about it."

"Yeah, she does." Emily let out an exaggerated laugh. "Boy, we almost got ourselves into a lot of trouble. So, Carl gave us this hammer, right?"

"Em..." Nickie glanced from Nathan to Laura and back again. *They're not even thinking about anybody else right now.*

"And he lent us this old book with a bunch of maps that —oh, crap. *That's* probably washed up somewhere at the Greenbelt right now. But the hammer belonged to a *dwarf,* Laura. And it really packed a—"

"Emily." Nickie raised her voice a little. "We can tell the story later."

Nathan unfolded his arms and pushed himself away

from the living room wall before slowly walking across the foyer toward Laura.

"Well, at least let me tell her about the Tree Folk." Emily rolled her eyes. "Because seriously, those guys showed up at the *perfect* time. We almost drowned!"

Nickie and Chuck had already sidled their way toward the dining room, trying not to laugh at Emily's complete obliviousness.

"Hey, where are you guys goin'? We still—woah." Emily stopped and blinked when she saw that Nathan had moved down the entire foyer toward Laura.

The physics professor didn't say a word before he grabbed the oldest Hadstrom witch's face in both hands and kissed her.

"Oh, okay. I guess you guys need a little time to—wow. You can't even hear me right now, can you?"

"Emily," Nickie called from the kitchen. "Now sounds like a really good time for a midnight snack or something."

"Hint taken. I'm gonna go cook something, so... Yeah." Emily pulled her gaze away from her oldest sister and the professor, who were making out against the front door. "And then I'll...whatever."

The youngest Hadstrom witch scurried out of the foyer, through the dining room, and into the kitchen. Chuck and Nickie stood side by side, leaning back against the counter by the sink and snickering.

"You couldn't have given me a little more of a warning or something?" Emily jerked her thumb behind her toward the front door.

"That's what I was trying to do, Em." Nickie laughed. "You were pretty caught up in trying to tell the story of how we broke into a Kashgar watchtower under the Greenbelt."

"Well, it's a *good* story." The youngest witch glanced quickly back at the front door, then rolled her eyes and headed right for the fridge. "They are *really* goin' at it."

"Maybe Laura's the kinda person who needs to be kidnapped by a witch-murderer to loosen up a little." When Nickie and Emily both stopped to shoot him identical incredulous looks, he shrugged. "Oh, come on. That's not something she does all the time."

Nickie laughed, grabbed her boyfriend's face, and gave him a kiss that was a lot less hot and heavy but still had plenty to say. "We can stop talking about Laura."

Emily pulled out a jar of strawberry jam and slammed it down on the counter beside the fridge. "As much as I love being the fifth wheel in my house, the kitchen's kinda my happy place. So, do you mind?"

"No problem." Chuck grinned at Nickie, gave her another quick peck on the lips, and pulled out a chair at the round kitchen table.

Nickie bit her lip and eyed the jar on the counter as Emily rummaged around through the fridge some more. "What are you gonna make with jelly?"

"I don't know." Emily shook her head, staring at the random things in their fridge. "Boy, having your sister kidnapped by the worst creature on this entire ship sure wipes grocery shopping right off the priorities list. Uh… how do you guys feel about PB&J? I guess."

"Well, *this* is new." Chuck rubbed his hand through his short blond hair and laughed. "The master chef wants to make us peanut butter and jelly sandwiches at ten o'clock at night."

Nickie sat next to him at the table and leaned back in her chair with her arms folded. "Sounds like the end of the world."

"Yeah, don't get your hopes up or anything." Emily grabbed the bag of sliced bread from the fridge, closed the door, and went to the pantry for the peanut butter. "The other option is 'everything in our fridge' stew. I'm gonna stick with keeping it simple right now."

"Hey, as long as you're making it, Em, I'm down." Chuck grinned. "Anything I can do to help?"

Right on cue, two pairs of footsteps moved up the staircase. The sound paused halfway to the second floor, and the stairs creaked. Holding out the jar of peanut butter like she intended to throw it instead of spread it, Emily glanced up at the ceiling. "Did she just...giggle?"

Nickie raised her eyebrows. "I didn't think Laura knew *how* to giggle."

Chuck burst out laughing and tried to cover it up with a fake cough.

The footsteps moved the rest of the way up the staircase and across the floor directly above the kitchen—which happened to be Laura's bedroom.

"So, part of me's really glad that's finally happening." Emily craned her neck and blinked up at the ceiling. "And I guess the other part of me expected them to be a little more..."

"Subtle? Private?" Nickie jumped in her chair when something fell over in Laura's bedroom and thumped onto the floor.

"Quiet, maybe?" The youngest Hadstrom sister shook her head.

Chuck cleared his throat and leaned forward over the table. "So, how 'bout those sandwiches, Em?"

"Yep." Emily gave them a dismissive wave and pulled a few plates down from the cabinet. The silverware drawer rattled and banged shut, and she got to work with the butter knife and her simple snack-making. "You guys go ahead and start talking about whatever. Try to be loud so I can focus."

"Huh. That's usually the other way around." Chuck leaned toward Nickie and wiggled his eyebrows. "Any chance you feel like pulling out your Strat and rocking out for however long Emily needs to *focus*?"

Nickie wrinkled her nose. "Can't."

"What? Since when did Austin's new Queen of Blues start saying she can't play?"

"Well...since I dropped my guitar to help Laura pin down the Gorafrex with a pointy iron stick before we rescued her a few hours ago. Then everything blew up."

Chuck shook his head in disbelief. "You *what?*"

"We'll get her a new one," Emily added, waving the jelly-covered knife around.

Something else crashed onto the floor of Laura's room above them, and Chuck pulled out his phone. "Okay. We'll go with someone else's music, then. Any requests?"

At the same time, the Hadstrom sisters in the kitchen both said, "Loud."

CHAPTER FOUR

With Jimmy Hendrix playing in the background slightly louder than necessary, Emily, Nickie, and Chuck were halfway through their sandwiches before Laura and Nathan all but ran down the stairs. Then Laura stormed through the dining room and into the kitchen.

Chuck almost choked on his bite of sandwich. "That was fast."

Nickie snorted.

Laura ignored them both. "You guys didn't think it was a good idea to tell me about my closet?"

Emily froze with her sandwich poised in front of her open mouth.

Nathan joined them in the kitchen, rubbing the back of his neck with an apologetic frown.

"Really?" Nickie turned halfway around in her chair to look at them. "That's what's on your mind right now?"

Laura gave her a blank look. "Should I be thinking about something else?"

Chuck sucked in a hissing breath through his teeth, then gestured toward the counter. "Emily made sandwiches..."

"Yeah, thanks." Nathan headed toward the extra plates and the leftover snacks Emily had so thoughtfully made for everyone.

"So, nobody's gonna say anything about what happened?" Laura folded her arms and glanced back and forth between her sisters.

"We were gonna tell you," Emily said, then went ahead and took that bite she'd put on hold. "Eventually."

"Laura, we just got back." Nickie shrugged a little and nodded toward the front door. "And you obviously needed a little time before we all sat down and filled each other in on everything that happened."

Chuck nodded. "So, if you need more time..."

"We're good." Nathan leaned back against the counter and ripped off a quarter of his sandwich with one bite.

Laura finally seemed to realize why the tension was suddenly so thick in the kitchen. "It's just...you know how many creatures I keep in there, right?"

"We sure do." Emily stuck her elbows on the table and kept chewing.

"And Nathan was in there with us yesterday to help us look for something to stick in the singing bowl," Nickie added. "You know, to find you."

"He was?" Laura blinked at the physics professor across the kitchen and started to blush again.

Nathan raised his eyebrows and took another huge bite of peanut butter and jelly.

"He pretty much refused to leave us alone until we figured out how to get to you. It was a little annoying, but eventually turned out to be exactly what we needed."

Emily grabbed the back of the table's last empty chair and pulled it out. "So, why don't you sit down and take a breather, huh? Want a sandwich?"

"Um..." Laura stared at the empty chair and tapped her fingers against her lips.

"Go ahead." Nathan grabbed the last plated sandwich off the counter and brought it to the table. He leaned toward Laura as he set down the plate and quickly kissed her temple. "I'm guessing that thing didn't think about feeding you, did it?"

Laura slowly sat in the last empty chair and reached out for the sandwich. "I wasn't really thinking about eating, either."

"That's a good start." Chuck pointed at her sandwich. "Emily makes a killer PB&J."

Emily scoffed. "It's a normal PB&J."

"Thanks." Laura took a small, hesitant bite, then sat back in her chair. "I'm sorry, guys. I know you did everything you could to get me out of there. And I really appreciate it."

"That's what we do, you know?" Emily shrugged. "When one of us gets kidnapped, we all work together to get them back."

"Here's to Laura being the only one of us who ever gets kidnapped." Chuck lifted the rest of his sandwich in a toast.

"Here's to Laura being the only one of us to get kidnapped and totally keep her cool while we try everything we can think of to find her." Nickie bumped her sandwich against Chuck's.

"You probably didn't need us, anyway," Emily added.

"Of course, I did." Laura took another bite. "I wouldn't have been able to keep the Gorafrex pinned like that for long. You showed up at the perfect time."

"You know, we tried to get there sooner," Emily said. "Things kept going wrong all over the place. I thought we broke the singing bowl at one point."

Laura choked on her food, coughed a little, and swallowed. "You didn't, though, right?"

"Pretty sure it's still in one piece," Nathan added. He'd returned to leaning against the counter and now licked peanut butter and jelly off his fingers. The sandwich was gone.

"We followed it to the apothecary, first." Nickie pushed her empty plate a few inches away and sat back in her chair with a laugh. "The singing bowl freaked out. We figured it was broken like everything else magic-related. Then it led us somewhere else."

"I *was* in the apothecary, though. For a while." Laura took another bite and gazed around the table.

"Yeah, we know."

"So, where did the bowl actually take you?"

Nathan chuckled. "To a wild pig."

"What?"

"A wild pig being chased by pink fireworks," Emily added.

The kitchen fell silent under the ridiculousness of their conversation, then all three Hadstrom sisters burst out laughing.

"Nathan was pretty disappointed," Nickie added.

The physics professor smirked. "I was, huh?"

"Yeah." Emily laughed again and pointed at him. "He was so gung-ho about coming with us to find you, and we ended up taking him on a wild pig chase. Like, literally."

"Okay, well, if that's supposed to be an embarrassing story about me, let's talk about that little silver hammer, Emily." Nathan cocked his head and grinned at her. "You were kinda disappointed about *that* one."

"Oh, so *now* you want me to tell it?" Emily looked from Nathan to Laura and back again. "You sure? I can wait if you guys need to go…clean up Laura's closet or something."

Laura stared at her. "Seriously?"

"*Or…*" Nickie stood and reached for all the empty plates on the table. "I could clean up after Emily's totally gourmet snack, then we can all sit and start filling in all the blanks from the beginning, right?"

She stacked the plates and took them to the sink. Emily and Laura both stood, and Chuck lifted his hands behind his head to lean back for a stretch.

"Sounds like a plan." Emily leaned toward Laura and muttered, "Do all those crazy creatures in your closet need you any time soon?"

"They're fine. I checked. It's a total mess in there, though."

"I know. I promise that wasn't us." Emily drew an X over her heart. "If you need any help in there tomorrow…"

"Thanks, Em. I'll let you know."

"Cool. Hey, the mop's still in the mudroom, right?"

"Already on it." Nathan stepped into the mudroom, a

few things clanged around, and then he walked right through into the living room with the mop and a bucket. "Chuck and I did manage to put the living room back together. Mostly."

Nickie's boyfriend pushed himself up out of his chair and puffed out a sigh. "Dave ruined it."

"Can't really blame him too much, though." Nickie wrapped her arm around Chuck as they headed after Nathan. "Can't really blame anybody right now for all the weird stuff going on."

Emily glanced at Laura and bared her teeth in a guilt-ridden grimace. "Except for us, right?"

"But we'll put everything back together, Em." Laura put her arm around her youngest sister's shoulders and walked with her into the living room—which was now charred halfway around with a giant puddle of rainwater still spreading out across the floor. "We're getting close."

"Yep. Still not done, yet."

"Um…" Nathan paused with the mop and stared at the puddle of water. "Is this something we should be worried about?"

Speed stood at the edge of the large puddle, lapping up the rainwater from Dave's unwieldy Peabrain spell. A ripple of electric-blue light pulsed away from the bulldog every time his tongue hit the water.

"Hey, Speed." Nickie bent beside the family pet and nudged the dog aside, first gently then with a little more force when Speed kept trying to get back to his convenient drink. "Look, you have a whole bowl full of water all to yourself. Get outta there."

"If a whole plate of chocolate cupcakes and a raging Gorafrex didn't stop him, I'm sure he'll be fine." Emily stared at the still-glowing water on their floor. "Right?"

Nathan chuckled and started mopping up the water. "Well, if he starts glowing, at least we'll know why."

CHAPTER FIVE

Nickie jolted awake in her bed the next morning with wide, wild eyes. It took her a few seconds to realize that the constant knocking, banging, and scraping she'd heard in her dream still surrounded her now after waking. "What *is* that?"

With a groan, she ran both hands through her hair and froze halfway through. There was that urgent, tribal drumbeat—faint but still completely familiar. The Gorafrex was drumming again, calling out to another witch or wizard to lure, capture, and drain for blood magic.

Nickie leapt out of bed, whipping the covers aside and struggling to free herself from the last folds twisted around her ankles without falling on her face. "Laura! Em! Something's wrong!"

Feet pounded toward her bedroom from both sides of the hall, and the door burst open with a loud bang. Laura hadn't bothered with her robe or slippers, and Emily hadn't changed out of her clothes after they'd passed out way too late last night.

"We hear it, too." Laura moved quickly toward Nickie, her keyring dangling from her outstretched fingers.

"But, we put it away." Nickie took a sharp breath, raised a hand to her temple, then froze. "No headache."

"Probably 'cause it's not in your head." Emily swirled her keyring around her finger and nodded toward Nickie's bedside table. "It's the Clubhouse coins."

"Huh?" Blinking heavily, Nickie turned toward her bedside table too and saw her set of keys lying there next to her phone, an empty glass, and a few extra guitar picks. The Gorafrex's ancient drumbeat stopped for a few seconds, then started up again in a short burst of pounding rhythm. Nickie's keys rattled against each other and the vibrating Clubhouse coin with her thumbprint etched into the silver surface. "It's still in there."

"As far as we can tell, yeah." Laura eyed the silver coin dangling from her keyring. "I honestly had no idea that was possible, but my guess is that sound is the only thing that can make it through."

"And it obviously won't be able to call any other witches or wizards." Emily went to join Nickie when the middle Hadstrom sister slowly sat on the edge of her bed. "Otherwise, you'd be having one serious migraine right now."

"Yeah." Nickie sighed, and the scattered drumbeat fell silent from all three Clubhouse coins. "How is that even possible?"

Her sisters shared a glance. Emily shrugged, and Laura shook her head. "It's probably something we missed when we built the Clubhouse in the first place. That's the part that's throwing me off right now."

"Laura, we made the Clubhouse like fifteen years ago. As *kids*." Emily dropped her keyring on Nickie's nightstand. "That's not exactly something we can blame ourselves for overlooking."

"Still." The oldest Hadstrom sister stared at her Clubhouse coin in one hand and tapped her lips with the other. "If there's a way for the drumbeat to get out, even if it's only sound, we need to make sure that nothing else has even the slightest chance of coming back through. Otherwise…"

"We're screwed?"

"Uh… Well, I wasn't gonna take it *that* far, Em. But sure. Something like that."

"We'd figure it out anyway." Nickie sighed and let out a relieved chuckle. "I'm really glad that's all it is, though. Just noise."

"Yeah, it kinda makes all the murdering, witch-killing, blood magic, and potentially destroyed Austin that much less…awful." Emily tilted her head from side to side. "Maybe more like trying to beat a videogame instead of trying to die or get kidnapped, right?"

Her sisters stared at her with blank expressions. Laura cleared her throat. "If that's what helps you compartmentalize this whole thing, Em, then sure. Just like a videogame in the contained dimension we made as kids. Totally."

"Just trying a different perspective." Emily shrugged. "How long do you guys think this—"

The Gorafrex's drumming started up again with a jolt, rattling both sets of keys on the nightstand and making all three Hadstrom sisters jump. After a few seconds, the sound slowly faded again.

"It's trying to get out," Laura said.

"So, we need to get to work with putting magic back together for everyone in Austin before we even think about getting that thing out of the Clubhouse and into the prison."

Emily cocked her head. "Guys? The drumming stopped."

"Yeah, Em. We noticed."

"So, what's still banging around downstairs?"

The scratching and knocking that had ripped Nickie right out of her sleep still rose from downstairs. "Speed, maybe?"

"Nickie, he has a dog door." Laura stared at the wall behind Nickie's bed and tried to focus on the sound. "And he'd have to have, like, a dozen front paws to make that kinda sound."

"He also doesn't scratch at the *front* door," Emily added. "That's where it's coming from."

Nickie stood from the bed and stormed across her room, rifling through the scattered piles of clothes until she found a pair of quarter-length joggers to slip on under her oversized Rolling Stones t-shirt. "Let's go figure out what the heck it is, then."

"Right."

The Hadstrom sisters left Nickie's room together and headed quickly but cautiously down the stairs to the first floor. The scratching and pounding and sharp, staccato ticks were definitely coming from the front door. A low whine rose behind them, and they turned around to find Speed sitting back on his haunches, staring at the front door, his head cocked in intense concentration.

"See?" Emily gestured toward their immortal family pet. "Not the dog."

"Have you guys ever seen him look this interested in anything?" Nickie crouched down in front of Speed and scratched behind his ears. "I mean, besides food."

Speed whined again and ducked his head away from Nickie's hand, his eyes still trained on the front door.

"And turning down the opportunity for attention and a good ear-scratch?" Emily shook her head. "No way."

Nickie tried to pet Speed again, but he let out another whine, took a few quick steps toward the door, and sat again. "All right, buddy. We'll check it out."

Laura went slowly toward the front door, grabbed the handle, and paused to look back over her shoulder. "You guys ready?"

"Yep."

"Open it."

The minute Laura opened the front door, a barrage of black feathers, beaks, and talons flooded into the Hadstrom sisters' house from the front stoop. Dozens of huge, mute, flightless grackles hopped and scrambled inside, funneling through the doorway and rushing right toward the witches.

"What the heck?" Emily tried to step back and almost stepped on one of the magical messengers madly fluttering its wings behind her. "It's only been a few days, birds. That's not enough time to turn a hundred grackles into domestic pets."

Laura let go of the door and pressed herself against the wall separating the foyer from the living room. "You guys didn't feed them while I was gone, did you?"

"Hey, these are wild birds," Nickie said, stepping carefully between ruffling feathers and beaks opening wide without any sound. "It's not our job to feed the messengers."

"It is when we're the ones who messed magic up so badly that the grackles are useless as messengers." Laura slowly turned to watch the huge blackbirds hopping against each other, fluttering over their fellows' heads, and milling around in general chaos. "It's our fault they can't fly or deliver their messages at all."

"Why were they trying to get inside?"

"Beats me, Em."

A few grackles stopped beside Speed, who sat patiently and didn't seem to care about the huge mass of birds in his house. The blackbirds cocked their heads at the immortal bulldog, ruffling their feathers, and opened their beaks. Of course, no sound came out. Speed's mouth dropped open to mock their soundless attempts, his tongue hanging over the end of his teeth.

"They obviously want *something*." Laura reached out for the open door and slowly shut it against the already unbearable summer humidity. The closest grackles hopped out of the way, apparently unconcerned by being shut up in the Hadstrom sisters' house. "I wish there was a way to—"

Another burst of the Gorafrex's frantic drumbeats rose from the keyring still in Laura's hand. This time, the ancient rhythm was accompanied by a bright silver light pulsing from the Clubhouse coin hanging beside her keys. A flutter of surprise and urgency rippled across the grackles gathered in the foyer. Those closest to Laura erupted into a flurry of beating wings and beaks snapping open and shut. A dozen of them turned toward her and hopped closer. Laura stepped back to press herself against the wall again.

"What did you do?"

"Nothing, Em." Laura lifted her hands and stared at the grackles hopping against each other and trying desperately to fly.

"Hey, did you see that your Clubhouse coin is flashing?" Nickie pointed.

"It's *what?*" Laura lowered her hand to stare at her keyring pulsing silver light and still emitting the urgent, sporadic drumbeat. "That's not supposed to happen. It's —hey!"

The grackles gathered around her legs had somehow managed to launch one of them high enough off the ground that the blackbird's open beak knocked against Laura's dangling keys. A second bird did the same, and then the oldest Hadstrom sister was penned in by a bunch of jumping birds, all snapping and fluttering at her keys.

"They know." Laura jerked away from another hopping blackbird. The next one that launched itself a few feet into the air managed to peck her wrist. "Ow!"

The keys fell from her hand, and the surrounding grackles darted toward them like they'd found food instead of a bunch of metal.

"They know what?" Nickie asked.

"That we put the Gorafrex in the Clubhouse. Look." Laura skirted around the grackles now that they ignored her completely. Those closest to her keys on the floor pecked desperately at the Clubhouse coin as it pulsed with silver light and sporadic drumbeats.

"I'm gonna agree with Laura on this one." Emily nudged Nickie's shoulder and pointed toward the staircase.

"Oh, jeeze." Nickie's eyes widened at the line of grackles fluttering and hopping up the staircase to the second floor. Something shattered at the end of the hall. "They're in my *room*."

"With our keys." Emily rushed up the stairs, dodging the chaotic blackbirds moving up the stairs. Nickie followed close behind.

When they stepped into Nickie's room, they found a dozen of the magical messengers flapping around on the bed. Two were already on the nightstand, both leaning over the edge and staring down at the handful of others pecking at Emily's and Nickie's Clubhouse coins pulsing the same light. They'd knocked the empty glass off, too, which now lay in scattered shards all over the floor.

"Okay, you guys need to stop." Nickie tried to step toward the grackles, but more kept flooding into her room and getting caught under her feet. "Seriously. Before one of you ends up eating a bunch of broken glass, or something."

"Everything okay up there?" Laura called from the foyer.

"Besides a hundred birds in our house making a mess out of everything?" Emily leapt away from the fluttering wings beating against her ankles. "Sure."

"They're attacking our coins up here, too, Laura." Nickie tried to step around the birds and realized there was a lot more glass on the floor than she thought. "We get it, birds. Nobody expects you to like the Gorafrex any more than we do."

The drumbeats finally fell silent from all three silver coins, and the pulsing lights faded away. The grackles flapped around a little more, but the pecking had stopped. A few seconds after that, the birds that had gathered around the fallen keys straightened, folded back their wings, and blinked at each other. The one closest to Emily looked up at her and hopped backward.

"Yep. Point taken."

The other birds turned toward Nickie and Emily and blinked their dark, beady eyes.

"Oh, *now* you wanna calm down and listen?" Nickie shot the birds a warning glance, then shook her head. "We get it."

The blackbirds hopped down off the bed and the nightstand, opening their beaks at the Hadstrom witches without any sound whatsoever. Then they formed a neat, straight line to hop, flutter, and waddle right out of the bedroom and back down the stairs.

Emily scratched her head. "I can't tell if they're annoyed with us or embarrassed."

"Probably a little of both."

Together, they followed the much calmer, almost civilized progression of grackles down the hall and the staircase toward the foyer. Laura looked up at them and shrugged. "Guess they don't like the drumbeats, either."

"That was pretty obvious. Oh. Excuse me." Emily lifted her foot and waited for the two grackles at the bottom of the stairs to hop aside so she could step into the foyer.

The blackbirds arranged themselves in a somewhat

neat fashion between the staircase and the front door, rustling black feathers and jostling each other enough to show that they weren't completely happy with the situation.

"We know we have to get the Gorafrex back into the prison," Laura told them. "The Clubhouse was only temporary because we didn't have any other options last night."

"But we'll take care of it," Emily added.

Nickie nodded and stepped off the last step, holding tightly to the banister in case any of the messengers slipped under her feet again. "That's a promise."

All at once, the nearly hundred blackbirds in the Hadstrom sisters' foyer lifted their wings a few inches and opened their beaks wide. Then every beak snapped shut again with one loud, echoing snap, and the grackles turned toward the door.

"Okay…" Laura opened the front door, and the birds hopped back outside in pairs. The sisters watched them make their way around the house to the side yard, which the grackles had turned into their temporary home since magic had all but stopped working completely.

"They're keeping an eye on us, aren't they?" Nickie leaned to the side to watch the last of the blackbirds disappear around the corner between the bushes.

"Snapped their beaks at us and everything." Emily shook her head in amazement. "Did that remind anyone else of Mom snapping her fingers to get us to be quiet when we were kids?"

"Or to pay attention. Yep." Laura closed the door and stared at it for a few seconds. "We got a slap on the wrist from a bunch of birds."

"Not the weirdest thing that's happened in the last few weeks."

"You know, Em, you're right." Laura blew a few strands of hair away from her forehead and turned back to face her sisters. "We have to get back to work."

"So much for having a little break, right?" Nickie shrugged. "I'll go make some coffee."

"Little break." Emily snorted and shook her head. "Says the new Queen of Blues who literally gets to make her own schedule."

"I'm pretty sure Chuck handles her scheduling, Em."

"Good thing the schedule's clear," Nickie called from the kitchen.

CHAPTER SIX

After a few cups of coffee, showers, and a frittata Emily put together from the rest of their eggs and the random ingredients still left in the fridge, the Hadstrom sisters sat down at the kitchen table to hash out their next moves.

"Rutilda said magic would only get worse until all the energy cores are destroyed." Laura tapped her lips a few times, then pointed at the map of central Austin she'd printed out. On that map, she'd drawn the wide circle running through the twelve black dots evenly spaced. Eleven of those dots were marked with a red X. Two of them were also circled in red. "The Gorafrex only got one and a half energy cores powered up, right?"

"And we destroyed both of them." Emily pointed to the last dot without an X. "So now we need to go bust out the last one, and we'll be good to start putting magic back together again."

Nickie crossed an ankle over her knee and folded her arms. "I sure hope so."

"Well, at the very least, we don't have to worry about the Gorafrex showing up while we go after the last energy core." Laura drained the last of her coffee. "So, we have a clear shot."

"For now." Nickie raised her eyebrows at the pile of all three sisters' keyrings in the center of the table. "We don't even know how long the Clubhouse can hold that thing."

"Guess we'll have to work fast and hope that we're lucky."

"Lucky? Really?" Emily blinked at her older sister and let out a wry laugh. "Since when does Dr. Laura Hadstrom believe in luck?"

"Since magic became completely unpredictable and more than a little dangerous, Em. Since our dog turned into a giant fighting machine and everything I thought I knew about how things work on this orbiting ship turned out to be a *guideline*." Laura stuck her finger down on the dot for the final energy core, which was right in the middle of a residential subdivision on the southwest end of Austin. "But I *do* know that we have to finish this and make sure that no part of that escape pod can ever be powered up or used again for anything."

"Sounds like you're expanding your mind a little." Emily grinned.

"Or, we can call it making our own luck."

"Then let's go make it and bash in the last energy core." Nickie slapped her hands down on the table and pushed herself to her feet. "Which means Emily needs to make more potions, right?"

"Yeah. I can definitely do that." Emily stood and quickly went into the dining room, which had become the center of operations in the Hadstrom sisters' house on Pressler Street. "You know, I think this is the first time that I've had all the ingredients we need and already know what potions to take with us."

"Look at that." Nickie chuckled. "This'll be almost as fast as it was before magic turned on us."

"Yeah, almost. Oh, crap." Emily whirled away from the table to peer into the kitchen. The clock over the stove read 8:13 a.m. "I'm covering closing shift tonight."

Laura eyed the messy array of potions ingredients on the dining room table, plus a pile of what looked like a soaking-wet dress halfway draped over a baking sheet. "I thought you only worked first shifts in the kitchen."

"Well, I *did*. Until I had to call in sick and switch shifts around so Nickie and I could track you down and make sure you didn't die." Emily reached across the table for the red plastic bucket she was currently using as a supply bin. She shrugged and absently dug through the assorted collection of potions vials before taking out a handful and setting them aside. "So now I have to keep up my end of things and close down the kitchen with everyone else tonight."

"What time do you have to go in?" Nickie slid the tin box of ingredients toward her, but Emily reached out and moved it back where she wanted it.

"Two o'clock. So, as long as we can get to the last energy core, blow it up, and not have to deal with anything else in the next six hours, I'll be fine."

"I think we can handle that." Nickie watched her little sister separate different ingredients based on some secret formula stashed only in Emily's head. "I thought being on the last shift through all of dinner was a pretty big deal at Meadowlark."

"Yep."

"So… why don't you look all that happy about it, Em?"

"Hey, can you grab me a few more bowls and a cup of water?" Emily looked up at her sister and pointed to the kitchen. "Like, eight ounces."

"And then you'll tell me why you're upset?"

"I'm not upset."

"Come on, Em." Laura stopped at the other end of the table and spread her arms. "We know you better than that."

"Bowls and water, please." Emily shot Nickie an incredibly fake grin, which disappeared the instant her sister turned into the kitchen to gather more potion-mixing supplies. "Okay, I'm not *upset*-upset. I just…"

"Don't wanna see John?" Laura offered.

"What? No, that's not—"

"Oh, yeah. Laura, we told him you were sick, by the way." Nickie came back into the dining room and set everything Emily wanted down on the table. "In case it comes up."

"Thanks for telling me. We can keep that a secret, Em. No problem. Don't let it keep you from how much you love your job."

"I'm not. It doesn't have anything to do with John."

"Right." Laura raised an eyebrow. "Just like you slamming everything across the living room with your leaky magic didn't have anything to do with John."

"A closing shift isn't remotely connected to him."

"Except for the fact that you and your boyfriend work together." Nickie frowned, then let out a surprised laugh.

"Actually, now that I think about it, we all work with our boyfriends."

"No, we—oh." Laura blinked and let out her chuckle of understanding. "Yeah, I guess we do. In different ways."

"Good to hear you finally admit that Nathan's your boyfriend." Emily smirked and poured equal amounts of water into four smaller mixing bowls.

"That's not what I said, Em."

"It totally is." Nickie drummed her fingers on the table and grinned at her older sister. "I'd say he earned it."

Laura snorted. "Why? Because he listened to the ground and found the old Kashgar watchtower under Barton Creek?"

Her sisters shared a glance and nodded. "Yep."

Nickie pointed across the table. "And because he read a bunch of Kashgar runes and got us into the secret room with the Isolation Vein. We literally wouldn't have been able to track you without him."

"Yes. Everybody made that perfectly clear last night." Laura folded her arms. "And nice try, by the way, but I'm not letting you change the subject, Em. We were talking about you and your issues with John."

"I don't have any issues with John!" The mostly empty measuring cup in Emily's hand slammed down on the dining room table, and the tiny bit of water left in there splashed out over her hand. She sighed, shook the water off onto the floor, and closed her eyes. "Okay, maybe we do have some issues. I don't know if I can date a guy who's had his memory wiped."

"It's for his good, Em." Nickie stepped closer and rubbed her little sister's back a few times. "The only reason

Chuck knows anything is because the Gorafrex tried to kill him. Me. Both of us. John got his memory cleaned up a little by that Huldu because that's what happens when humans see something they're not supposed to."

Emily grew rigid under her sister's hand, so Nickie calmly pulled away. "He would've been able to handle it."

Nickie and Laura shared a glance. "Probably, yeah."

"And he should've been offered a choice, at least. Or the Huldu could've asked *me* first. We would've handled it."

"I know, Em."

"And I don't even know if John's working tonight, so that doesn't matter." Emily grabbed a bundle of dried stems that were a dull brown-green at one end and a milky-white on the other. She pulled half the stalks away and folded the ends together, crushing them between her hands and sprinkling the sour-smelling dust into one of the bowls.

"So…you don't like working at Meadowlark anymore, or…"

"You guys won't let it go, will you?" The youngest Hadstrom sister let out a sarcastic, humorless laugh. "I didn't *earn* working a closing shift. That's the issue. I only got it in trade because another chef picked up for me yesterday. Not on merit. So, they're gonna stick me in a corner that doesn't get any action, and it'll be a waste of my skills, and I'd lose any opportunity to do something bigger and better."

"Oh." Laura cocked her head and glanced around the dining room, trying to find something else to say that didn't make her sound so speechless.

Emily scoffed. "It would be like someone asking you to

sub one of their advanced classes, Laura. By playing *The Mummy* or something."

"Hey, that's a good one." Nickie grinned.

"Not the worst movie," Laura added, her eyes wide. "Totally horrifying thought. I'd never play a movie for someone else's class."

"Well, if I don't show up to work, I lose all my credibility. Used up my one chance to come save *you* from certain death-by-Gorafrex." Emily tossed her hand across the table toward Laura. "You're welcome."

"You know what, Em?" Laura shot her little sister a reassuring smile, shaking a finger at Emily. "You're gonna blow everyone in that kitchen away tonight. They know you're good. And you beat the system to get one of these shifts earlier and show them all what you can really do."

"I appreciate your attempted encouragement." Emily quickly glanced up at the baking sheet and supplies she and Nickie had left out last night in lieu of saving Laura from her Gorafrex kidnapper. "Hey, could you dump out that big bowl for me? I'm gonna make extra explosive potions."

Nickie snickered.

"Yeah, okay, Em." Laura reached for the bowl on the baking tray, which was still half-filled with dark blue tracking potion. She paused, blinked rapidly, and gingerly reached out to pinch a little of the damp black fabric piled on the tray and spilling over the end of the table. "Did you guys…is this my *graduation gown*?"

"What?" Emily jerked her head up from the barely started potions and blinked. "I mean…"

Nickie cleared her throat. "We needed something for the singing bowl, Laura. You know, something personal."

"I thought Inéz got it." Laura sniffed at the damp fabric and quickly pulled away. "What *is* this?"

"Tracking potion." Emily shrugged. "We had to make one after the singing bowl went nuts. Which was really the Gorafrex's wards leading us away from Brightwing Emporium."

"Did it work, at least?"

"Well, we did get *a* tracking potion to work." Nickie looked at her little sister for backup.

"And *that* one definitely worked. Just not the whole cap-and-gown bit. Sorry." Emily grimaced, and both younger Hadstrom sisters waited tensely for Laura to explode.

Instead, their sister made a disgusted face at the garment and drew it slowly off the table. When she held it up in front of her, the charred holes from Emily's first tracking spell gone haywire were perfectly clear. "I know why she did this."

Emily decided to act like this wasn't being made into a big deal and instead tried to focus on their potions. "Uh...who?"

"Inéz. She's angry at me for having left everyone in their pens without any supervision. Or food."

Nickie swallowed. "And you're reading angry gorlek off that thing?"

"Look at it, Nickie. It's charred all over." Laura held the gown up even higher, stretching her arms above her head to their fullest extent, and peered through the singed hole in the center of the black fabric. "Burned right through. I mean, I thought Inéz and I had an understanding about this kinda thing, but maybe it's the broken magic that's getting to her."

"An understanding." Nickie nodded slowly.

"Yeah. A gorlek lighting things on fire is like a cat peeing all over the place. I'll have to go remind her who's in charge here, and we'll be fine again."

Emily snorted. "Good luck. Have you *seen* that giant fire-breathing slug with a beak lately?"

Laura tossed her graduation gown back onto the table and stuck her hands on her hips. "Yeah, actually. Last night. She about knocked the closet door off its hinges."

"Oh..." Emily nodded. "*That's* what interrupted you guys."

"What are you talking about?"

"Nothing." Nickie shook her head at Emily with wide eyes. "Is Inéz still...you know. Giant?"

"Well, yeah. That's one of the first things we'll have to deal with once we get rid of this last energy core and start putting magic back together the right way." Laura smirked and looked back and forth between her sisters. "And yes, I said *we*. Nathan told me all about the three of you going through the stuff in my museum and making all the animals freak out. So, you can help me clean up *that* mess, too."

Emily pressed her lips together and fought back a laugh.

"Emily."

"Yeah."

"What's so funny?"

The youngest Hadstrom sister shook her head, although a tiny chuckle still escaped through her nose. "Nothing."

Laura stepped toward her, smiling in a mixture of

curiosity and disbelief. "Come on. You're bursting at the seams here. Just say it."

"I…didn't know you and Nathan went up to your room last night to talk about a bunch of magical creatures in your closet. That's all."

Nickie coughed to cover up her laugh. "I'm thirsty. You guys want some water?"

Her sisters ignored her.

"Okay, Em. Not sure what you're implying here, but it's probably better if you focus on your potions. And I'll go look for something we can use as a responsible way to carry them around without breaking them all this time." With a flashing grin and a seemingly innocent flutter of her eyelashes, Laura turned from the dining room table and headed into the foyer.

The old Victorian house groaned around them. Walls shifted down into place on the other side of the living room as the staircase folded in on itself and receded into the shape of whichever magical room Laura wanted to visit next. Nickie leaned against the entryway into the kitchen and folded her arms. "You *almost* managed not to say anything this time, Em."

"I tried. She kept pushing."

"That's what Laura does."

Emily chuckled and picked up the next bundle of ingredients for her bulk batch of explosive potions. "Not sure what I'm implying… Yeah, right. She knows exactly what I was talking about."

CHAPTER SEVEN

An hour later, Emily had finished making her potions, Nickie had finished cleaning up after her, and Laura stepped back into the dining room after the foyer had finished reassembling the house around her.

"How's it comin', Em?" The oldest Hadstrom sister stepped into the dining room and slipped the straps of a massive trekking pack off her shoulder.

"All done." Emily dusted off her hands and spread them in front of the table. "We got triple servings of the super awesome explosives I haven't gotten to try out nearly as much as I wanted. Some backup teleportation potions. You know, to get us home again. The Clubhouse is off-limits, for obvious reasons. And…oh, yeah. A little extra healing juice. I mean, we have the sister-jumping-cables goin' for us, so Nickie shouldn't have any problem with her awesome healing magic. If we even need to use it. Plus, everything else we've known we needed and still haven't been able to use."

Laura blinked and shook her head a little. "You're

gonna have to remind us of those. You've made a *lot* of potions in the last few days."

Emily grinned. "I really have, haven't I?"

Nickie pointed to the other assorted colors of vialed and stoppered potions. "That's the…return potion, or whatever it's called. The one that'll take the Gorafrex out of the host it's in."

"Yep." Emily folded her arms.

"And this silver one is the binding potion, right?"

Laura raised her eyebrows. "Binding?"

"You really haven't put that one together yet?" When Emily turned toward her oldest sister and saw the complete lack of recognition on Laura's face, her jaw dropped. "Seriously? Laura, we went all the way to the Greenbelt and chiseled off a piece of the Isolation Vein for this. I mean, it was to find *you*. And your ring. But still."

"That…" Laura pointed as the swirling silvery potion that looked like watered-down mercury. "That's to put the Gorafrex back inside the prison."

"Bingo!" Nickie shot her big sister the guns.

"We used it to track your ring, because…*ta-da*. The Hadstrom rings were made from the same vein of iron that apparently built the prison, too. So, it's only a matter of timing at this point. Stab that thing with the lance again. We already know the rune works to transport it. Then hit it with potion number one to get the Gorafrex out of its stolen Peabrain suit, and bam. Toss the Isolation Vein potion right at its weird, shimmering, bodiless form. Should go right back to the prison after that."

"That's one too many shoulds, Em."

"Oh, come on." Nickie stepped around the table and

gave Laura's shoulder a little shake. "Emily has this *down*. If it involves potions, it works every time."

"Almost," Emily muttered.

"What?"

"What? Nothing." The youngest Hadstrom sister glanced at the other end of the dining room table, but the mess of Laura's ruined graduation gown had already been cleared away. "I know what I'm doing."

"I know you do."

"So…" Nickie gestured toward the giant trekking pack Laura had lugged through their house and onto the table. "What's with the hiking gear?"

"Not for hiking." Laura unzipped the pack and pulled out a metal lockbox that filled the entire pack with very little room for anything else. "I was busy, too."

She set the lockbox on the table and lifted the metal latches keeping the lid clamped down. When Laura pulled back the lid and let it drop all the way, she stood back and grinned.

"You built a…" Emily cocked her head. "Spill-proof carton for tiny eggs."

"What? No, Em." The oldest Hadstrom sister reached across the table and picked up one of the finished potions vials. The vial wedged snugly inside one of the few dozen depressions in the foam padding lining the lockbox. "Potions vault. How 'bout *that*?"

"Wow." Emily laughed. "That's actually…yeah. Pretty good."

"You didn't use any magic for this, did you?" Nickie poked at the foam, then tried to peel it away from the edge of the metal box.

Laura swatted her sister's hand aside. "No, I didn't use any magic. Because you two weren't with me, and I'm not an idiot."

"But you're pretty handy with a hot-glue gun." Nickie nodded and stuck out her bottom lip. "Good work."

"Thank you."

"There's one little problem with this, though." Emily gestured to the lockbox, then the trekking pack. "What happens if we need one of these potions like two seconds ago? Someone has to take out the box, open it, and find the right potion. It's not exactly magic-quick."

"Well, it's faster than having no potions left at all when crazy magic tosses us all over the place and the vials break in your fishing vest."

Emily rolled her hand toward her oldest sister in a little bow. "Touché."

"Plus, it's not like we have to fight anything right now at the last energy core. The Gorafrex is…temporarily detained."

Nickie pursed her lips. "Yeah, but we didn't have to *fight* anything to get out of the last chamber once we sent the Gorafrex to the Clubhouse. And that was still hard enough to do without getting blown up or tossed through a stone wall or something."

Laura pointed at the finished potions vials. "Let's focus on one thing at a time, huh? Vials in the box. And we'll figure out how to handle the rest when we're standing in front of that last energy core, okay?"

"Aye-aye, Dr. Hadstrom." Emily squinted with one eye closed and gave Laura what was probably meant to be a salute.

"What are you doing?"

"Agreeing with you." Laughing, the youngest Hadstrom sister picked up her vials and organized them by color and danger level inside the foam padding of the lockbox. "Were you planning on doing a lot of hiking to get to this energy core?"

"No. It's the biggest bag I have." Laura gave the empty trekking pack a loving pat. "This thing has been with me in the field for more discoveries at more sites than I can count."

"Oh." Nickie grabbed the pack and gave it a playful little shake. "This is your super fancy *archaeologist* pack, huh?"

"It's an Osprey," Laura shot back. "Trust me, this thing can handle whatever that old Velikan technology can throw our way."

"Looks like we have a few theories to test out with this one."

Emily closed the lockbox and handed it over to Laura to be slid back into the pack and zipped up tightly. "Let's go finish this."

She spun away from the dining room table and marched into the foyer. Nickie laughed, and Laura hurriedly zipped up the pack again before slinging it over her shoulder. "Em, you know we're not done after we break the last energy core, right?"

"You know what I mean." The front door opened, and the Hadstrom sisters stepped out into the late-morning heat of a summer day in Austin.

CHAPTER EIGHT

The drive to Circle C Ranch took them an uninterrupted fifteen minutes. The neighborhood was a nice subdivision on the southwest side of Austin, right off Highway 290. And then things started to get weird.

In the back seat of Nickie's car, Emily leaned forward over the center console and pointed at the windshield. "Are you guys seeing this?"

"Yeah, Em." Laura squinted down the street, then looked out her window on the passenger side and clicked her tongue. "I wonder how many other people right now are seeing a bunch of neighborhood trees glowing bright blue."

"Doesn't look like a lot." Nickie slowed her car to a crawl and looked out her window, ducking to catch a glimpse of the tips of the trees in the front yards. "Most people are out at work, right?"

"Most people with nine-to-five jobs, maybe." Laura

shook her head. "I wouldn't say that's most people in Austin."

"Maybe it's most people in this neighborhood?" Emily wrinkled her nose. "Could go either way, really."

"Well, we can take it as a good sign that nobody's running around capturing all the glowing trees on live video or anything." Laura shrugged. "At least, not yet."

Nickie pulled over at the corner of Beachmont Lane and Bexley Lane and turned off the engine. "Looks like it's only right here in the neighborhood, though. So, it's because of the energy core, right?"

"That, and the fact that we basically brought the Gorafrex with us." Emily pulled her keyring out of her back pocket and dangled it in front of her before sliding back against the seat. "No drums or flashing lights, though."

"I'm sure the ship knows by now that the Gorafrex is responsible for all the magic going haywire." Laura patted her keyring in the side pocket of her cargo shorts. "Or at least, the sentient parts of the ship in Austin. The trees want us to lock that thing up as much as we do."

"I didn't know you were an expert on trees." Nickie smirked at her big sister and pulled her keys out of the ignition.

"Yeah, well, I'm not. But I *did* learn a lot about this ship and the way it all works together when Nathan and I were going through that old Kashgar book of runes."

"Oh, *Nathan…*" Emily let out a little chuckle and shook her head. "Should we have called him for this?"

"Definitely not." Laura unbuckled her seatbelt and opened the passenger-side door. "He did his part by helping you guys get the original iron so you could find *me*. But this stuff with the energy cores is our mess. Our responsibility."

"Okee-doke." Emily hopped out of the back seat and quickly popped open the trunk. "Laura, you were planning on wearing this thing anyway, right?"

"Oh, yeah." Both front doors of Nickie's car closed. "I'm the only person who gets to wear that thing."

"Well, here you go." Emily closed the trunk again and handed the trekking pack with their securely fastened potions to her sister. "Now. Where's this energy core?"

"Somewhere in the neighborhood." Laura strapped the pack over her shoulders and fastened the buttons around her midsection. "Wanna try for a transport bubble?"

"If it was good enough for most of the others, it's gotta be good enough for this one." Nickie shrugged and reached out for each of her sisters' hands. "Let's power up some Hadstrom magic."

Laura snorted and grabbed Nickie's hand. "Okay. Let's make this—"

The trees in the corner yard groaned behind the Hadstrom sisters. All three of them jumped and stepped away from the car and the yard until they stood almost in the middle of the empty street. One huge poplar growing beside the corner house creaked and snapped, bending in the middle where the branches split off from the trunk and reaching toward the three witches in the street. This one was glowing, too, sending bright flashes of blue bursts up from the roots and into the outstretched branches.

"Great." Nickie blinked and studied the tree that shouldn't have been able to move like that on its own, especially without so much as a breeze. "First the grackles, now the trees. Don't they know we're already trying?"

"Maybe that's it, though." Emily pointed at the trees. "The grackles were trying to get our attention about the Clubhouse coins. What if the trees know, too? And they know that we're here for the energy core?"

"And then what, Em?" Laura scoffed at her youngest sister and tossed a hand in the air. "The trees want us to follow them? It's probably a little more complicated than—"

The trees groaned again, branches rustling and stirring almost violently on the silent neighborhood street. Except it wasn't just the glowing tree closest to the Hadstrom sisters. It was all of them. Every tree lining Beachmont—and Bexley, as far as they could see—now pulsed in constantly streaking blue light. The closest tree bent in the opposite direction, sending a shiver of loose leaves down to the yard as the wood creaked and snapped. The next tree over did the same, followed by the next two on the other side of the cross street.

Nickie ran a hand through her hair and shot Laura a sideways glance. "You were saying?"

"Okay, so they're bending in one direction away from us." Laura gripped the straps of her trekking pack and took off down the street toward the last of the unnaturally bent trees. "It's still not *literally* following the trees. They can't just unroot themselves and walk us down the street."

"Never say never," Emily muttered, staring at the glowing blue trees all around them. "That would be pretty cool."

"Let's work with what we have so far, Em." Laura led

her sisters down Bexley Lane toward the last bent trees. When the Hadstrom sisters reached those, a few more on both sides of the street groaned and stretched farther in the same direction. "Okay. They definitely want us to follow."

Nickie laughed. "I wanna see how these trees are gonna lead us underground to the energy core."

"Oh, hey." Emily jogged a little to catch up with her sisters. "Remember that story Dad used to tell when we were really little?"

When she didn't say anything more than that, Nickie shot her little sister a frown over her shoulder. "That narrows it down to every story Dad's ever told us."

"No, I mean the one about the oldest on Arenya V, right? The one that was sort of like...I don't know. Some type of consciousness for all the trees, everywhere."

"I still don't see where you're trying to go with this, Em."

"The *wizard*, you guys." Emily rolled her eyes and put a hand on each of her sisters' shoulders. "The wizard wanted to find...what was it? Some potion for eternal life or something."

Nickie nodded. "And the tree wrapped him up in its branches and pulled him underground."

"Yeah, Em, there are a couple holes in that story. Which is also just a story."

"Oh, yeah? Like what?"

Laura quickly glanced back at her and shot her an amazed smile. "Okay, for one, it was a bedtime story. Second, it's a bedtime story about trees on Arenya V, not on this ship. And then there's the whole part about how the tree showed the wizard that eternal life already existed in magic and the connection between all living things, but he wasn't gonna get a potion because he didn't *own* life any more than every other creature or lifeform on the planet."

"Wait. No..." Emily frowned. "That's not how the story ends."

"It is, Em." Nickie shrugged. "Dad told Laura and me that story hundreds of times when you were born. I think by the time you got here, he was tired of making his kids cry with a disappointing ending."

"What?" The youngest witch stopped and stared straight ahead as her sisters kept moving toward the farthest bent trees.

"Count yourself lucky, Em. That fake ending saved you hours of lying awake in bed wishing that wizard got his potion so he could...what was it?"

"I think he was trying to save his brother or something," Nickie offered.

"I can't believe he did that." Emily shook her head and caught up to her sisters. "Dad and I are gonna have a talk about this. What other lies of my childhood do I need to be aware of before I shove it all in his face?"

"Uh..." Nickie laughed. "You should probably ask Dad."

"My whole worldview's gonna turn upside down."

"Hey, it's not the end of the world, Em. Think of it like this." Laura eyed the rustling branches of the glowing tree they passed now just in front of a pastel-purple house. "You got the happiest childhood out of all three of us."

"My childhood was a lie..." Emily rubbed her hands down her cheeks and let out a massive sigh.

"Head in the game, Em." Nickie reached back to nudge

her little sister's shoulder. "Any minute now, we're gonna have to—"

"Watch out!"

"Well, yeah. When we reach the energy core—"

"No, I mean—" Emily grabbed Nickie's arm and the top of Laura's trekking pack and pulled them both onto the sidewalk with her as a huge shadow darted across the street and barreled through the space where they'd just been standing.

"What the heck is *that*?" Nickie spun around to find the streaking shadow again.

"More birds." Laura squinted. "They're obviously not grackles."

"No, those are a bunch of barn swallows. Flying upside-down." Wrinkling her nose, Emily squinted at the huge flock of tiny colorful birds as they wheeled around in the sky and came back toward the Hadstrom sisters. "What are they doing?"

The birds flapped around in a hectic, chaotic cloud and tried landing on one of the glowing blue trees. The topmost branches reached out lightning-quick and snatched up a quarter of the flock before falling still again.

"Please tell me the trees aren't eating birds now," Emily whispered.

"The trees aren't eating birds, Em." Nickie started walking backward. "If those were even birds. We should keep going."

They followed the next bending, flashing trees past a few more houses down the street and came to a small empty lot overgrown with weeds. The tall stalks rustled and waved around, and Emily leapt away from the edge of the unkempt yard. "What—"

Two huge koi fish flopped and jumped and wiggled out of the weeds, somehow making their way across the sidewalk and onto Emily's shoes. She quickly stepped back and pointed. "Fish out of water."

"Huh…" Laura frowned. "Anything else in that lot?"

"How am I supposed to know?" Emily stepped away from the weeds and shook her head. "And before you say it, I'm not a big fan of diving through all those overgrown weeds to find out."

"Woah!" Nickie doubled over and ran her hands frantically over her scalp, shaking out her hair.

"Nickie?"

"There's something in my hair."

"What?"

"I felt it! Crawling on my head." Nickie shook out her hair even more, and sure enough, something dropped out of her thick, dark-brown locks and smacked onto the sidewalk.

"Okay." Emily blinked in surprise and cocked her head. "That's a beetle the size of your shoe."

"Gross." The thought of that thing being in her hair made Nickie shiver, and she rolled her shoulders back to try pushing the creepiness aside. "Are there normally beetles this size in Austin?"

"Nope." Laura squatted in front of the huge black carapace that shimmered with blue and purple under different angles. She grabbed a twig off the sidewalk and brought slowly toward the massive insect. "This looks like a—"

The minute the stick touched the grotesquely large

pincers, the beetle let out a loud, violent hiss and burst into dozens of tiny, bright orange butterflies. Laura fell backward out of her squat, and the butterflies knocked against each other repeatedly before half of them fell to the street as a bunch of tiny white pebbles. The other half flew away.

"Magic needs to start doing its job again," Laura muttered, pushing herself to her feet and dusting off her cargo shorts. "Sooner rather than later."

"Maybe we should ditch the whole 'follow the trees' idea and cast a transport bubble to the energy core." Nickie shrugged. "This feels totally weird."

"I agree about the weird part." Laura gestured toward the trees. "But we can't simply ignore whatever those trees are trying to show us. Remember when the Gorafrex was still...using Dave as a host? We stopped it then, and the trees *did* something. Didn't they?"

"I have no idea. I was too busy shredding my guitar with a tiny amp and trying to play that lullaby nonstop so that thing couldn't get into my head and make it explode." Nickie shot her sister a pert look. "And it would be totally cool if we could make sure we never have a repeat of that particular energy-core-destroying session."

"Let's see where the trees lead, okay? If it's a dead end, we'll go with the transport bub—" Laura slapped her hand against the side pocket of her cargo shorts and froze in surprise. The Gorafrex's ancient, tribal drumbeat had started again. "You guys can hear that, right?"

"I can feel it, too." Emily had her hand pressed against the back pocket of her jeans where she'd stuck her keyring. "Like a private Gorafrex phone line."

The trees closest to the Hadstrom sisters on the street

rustled even more violently, shivering all the way down to the roots until the sidewalk trembled. A few cracks split the cement, and Nickie shook her head. "This isn't good."

Emily looked up at the house on the other side of the vacant lot and pointed. "Neither is that."

CHAPTER NINE

A wizard in his late thirties stood behind the open front door of his house on Bexley Lane, staring at the three Hadstrom witches hanging out on the sidewalk.

"Hey, there." Laura lifted a hand in a friendly wave. "How's it goin'?"

The wizard squinted at them, glanced across the street, then slipped out onto the front porch without bothering to shut the door. "I've been hearing some weird noises all morning. Do you… I know this probably sounds crazy—"

"Don't worry about it," Emily said with a reassuring smile. "Everything right now sounds and looks and feels crazy, huh?"

"Yeah." The wizard sighed and stepped off his front porch, rubbing his bright orange hair and squinting against the sun. "Thing is, I thought I just felt an earthquake. We haven't had anything like that around here, so I'm not sure. You all heard about the Peabrain that blew up his back yard last week, right?"

"The kid?" Nickie nodded and tried not to look like she

knew any more than this concerned magical citizen. "Yeah, we heard about that."

"Weird, right? You haven't seen anything like that around here, have you?" The man reached the end of his driveway and turned toward the Hadstrom sisters on the sidewalk. "I'm trying to keep my family safe, you know? We just had a kid."

"Hey, congrats." Emily's grin faded quickly when the man's concerned frown didn't let up at all.

"We can't stay in the neighborhood if there's…if there's a…when it…" The ginger wizard blinked lazily, his eyes opening again at different times as if they'd been completely disconnected. He stopped a few yards away from the Hadstrom sisters and slowly tilted his head, staring slack-jawed at the space right beyond the three witches in front of him.

"Um…sir?" Laura stepped toward him and leaned forward, waving her hand in a wide arc. The wizard didn't blink at all this time.

"Is he okay?" Emily stepped off the sidewalk to move in a wide circle around the frozen wizard.

"Doesn't really look like it, Em." Nickie frowned. "Let's keep going. He'll snap out of it."

The sisters moved cautiously down the sidewalk now, still following the bent trees.

"Oh, hey. No Gorafrex drums. That's nice." Emily patted her back pocket and pointed at the next few trees bending down the street where the Hadstrom witches were already headed. "So, we follow the trail of glowing blue—"

"Jeeze!" Nickie jumped and pulled her keyring out of

her pocket. The tribal drumbeat rose again even louder from the Clubhouse coin dangling beside her keys, but it wasn't anywhere near as loud as getting up close and personal with the bodiless witch-hunter. Or when Nickie could hear it in her head. "This is getting *really* annoying."

"Maybe clip it to your belt loop." Emily followed her own suggestion and wiggled her hips a little. The keys jingled against the Clubhouse coin now pulsing with silver light and letting out pounding, rhythmic beats rising and falling in volume. "Can't even feel it now."

The trees creaked and groaned all around them, and now even the branches that had bent and swayed to lead the Hadstrom sisters forward snapped back into their original positions.

"Emily," Laura muttered, reaching out for her youngest sister's beltloop as she stared across the street. "I think we should keep our keys in our pockets. Or at least not hanging out in the open."

"Why? It's not like the coins can actually *do* anything. Honestly, it just looks like a light-up speaker or something. Who's gonna notice?" Emily glanced up at Laura, then followed her sister's gaze across the street. "Oh..."

"I think lots of people have noticed, Em." Nickie slowly stuck her keyring back into her pocket and turned around. "There are a *lot* of witches and wizards in this neighborhood."

Laura tightened her grip on the straps of her trekking pack. "And they all hear the drums."

"Wait, I thought the drums had totally lost their power when they're...leaking out of the Clubhouse." Emily backed away from the street, moving her gaze from one open front door and blindly shuffling witch or wizard to the next. "Still no headache, right, Nickie?"

"Still no headache." Nickie took a quick step back when the ginger wizard took a slow, brain-addled step toward her. "But we're not exactly regular witches, either."

"They're not gonna do anything." Laura nodded down the street in the direction the trees had previously been leading them. "If the Gorafrex had physically been in this neighborhood instead of in our Clubhouse, the same thing would happen."

"It turns our whole race into zombies…"

"Yeah, Em. Minus the whole eating people part. Come on." Laura grabbed Emily's wrist and pulled her farther down the sidewalk. "Nickie, let's go."

"We were supposed to get rid of this last energy core quick and easy." Nickie backed away from the ginger wizard and finally turned to jog toward her sisters again. "This isn't either of those things. It's not particularly anonymous, either."

"But it's not dangerous."

"Yeah, for *us*, maybe. Laura, what about them?"

The oldest Hadstrom sister shrugged and stared up at the trees. "They're not hurting themselves or us or anyone else. My guess is they're following the drumbeats, and when it stops, they'll forget all about it. Okay, trees. We're ready to follow again, so…any time now."

"Laura's talking to *trees* now." Emily let out a nervous chuckle and stared up at the glowing blue branches too. "That's new."

"They obviously had something to say, Em." Laura headed across the closest lawn toward the shimmering blue trunk of a large live oak. "I'm trying to show up and listen. We all should."

"I really don't like this." Nickie caught up to her sisters again. "Let's go with the transport bubble, huh? That's way less of a headache. And not nearly as creepy."

Laura reached out to press her hand against the live oak's trunk pulsing with light. "Just a little longer."

None of them noticed the Gorafrex's ancient, magical-luring drumming had stopped echoing from their Clubhouse coins until Bexley Lane erupted with gasps, hesitant whispers, and a few startled shouts.

"What's going on?"

"Did you feel that?"

"Harry? Why are you standing in the middle of the street in your boxers?"

The unmistakably shrill cry of an infant rose from a few houses down. "Oh, my God." The ginger wizard whirled around and darted back down the sidewalk. He left the door open again when he rushed back into his house, but a few seconds after that, the baby stopped crying.

"We're doing the Gorafrex's work *for* it, Laura," Nickie whispered, leaning toward her sister.

"No, we're not. That thing can't get out of the Clubhouse. Not yet."

"But it's *trying*. What happens if it gets out, huh?" Nickie grabbed her big sister's hand and pulled it off the tree. "Laura, if it escapes, it's coming out of our coins. And we pulled every witch and wizard on this street out of their houses. Against their will."

"Who are all going back inside, by the way." Emily jerked her head toward the street. "So, I think we're okay."

"Why did the trees stop moving?" Laura frowned up at the glowing bark and shook her head. "I don't get it."

"That's a puzzle we can solve a little later." With a firm grip on Laura's wrist, Nickie extended her other hand toward Emily. "Transport bubble. Energy core. Right now."

"Sounds good to me." Emily took her sister's hand and nodded. "Go for it."

Nickie nodded, but then the Gorafrex's drumming returned, and it sounded louder. "What's it *doing* in there?

"Trying to get out, Nickie. Oh." Laura looked away from the tree and at her sisters with wide eyes.

"See, when *I* do that, it means I had a really good idea." Emily licked her lips. "When you do it, it means something's wrong."

Laura leaned toward her sisters and whispered, "Do we know if magic still works *inside* the Clubhouse?"

"Do we—*what?*" Nickie glanced over her shoulder at the witches and wizards shuffling back toward the Hadstrom witches again, caught once more under the Gorafrex's luring call. "Laura, please don't say you asked us that question without actually knowing the answer."

"Why would I ask if I knew the answer?" Laura clenched her eyes shut and grunted in frustration. "I didn't even think about the fact that a different dimension *might* not be affected by the crazy magic in Austin."

"Well, is it?" Emily stared at the witch limping toward them down the sidewalk. The woman had apparently been about to slip on her other heel before the drumbeats started again. Now she hobbled up and down on one three-inch heel and one bare foot. "Laura, does magic still work in the Clubhouse?"

"I don't *know*!" Laura clenched her eyes shut again and muttered something neither of her sisters could hear.

"What?"

"When I used the coin at Brightwing Emporium, I left you guys a note."

"Yeah. Origami jellyfish." Nickie nodded. "So?"

"It was still flying around when I grabbed it."

"Is that enough magic for the Gorafrex to do something really awful?" Emily thrust her head toward her sister and raised her voice. "Like maybe break out?"

"I have no idea, Em. But it's a lot more magic than any of us realized when we put that thing in our secret hideout without really thinking about it." Laura nodded at Nickie. "So yeah, let's go with the transport bubble."

Laura took each of her sisters' hands, and Nickie lifted her hand to focus on her black legacy ring. "Thinking about the energy-core chamber. That's it."

"Ow!" Emily jerked away from Laura but didn't let go of her sister's hands. She leaned sideways and glared down at the keyring hanging from her hip. "What the heck?"

"Em? What's—oh, *jeeze*!" Laura had to let go of Nickie's hand to rip her own keyring out of her shorts' side pocket. Nickie wasn't far behind her in pulling her keys from her back pocket with a yelp.

"Hot coins, huh?" Glaring at the pulsing silver light on her Clubhouse coin, Nickie held her keys out in front of her and shook her head. "I really hope that's as bad as it gets. Let's try again."

The Hadstrom sisters rearranged themselves so they

could still power up a real spell together without any of their Clubhouse coins burning holes through pockets or pants or skin. Nickie's black legacy ring flashed, and an opalescent bubble formed on the tip of the band. It grew slowly, then started to shrink.

"Nope." Emily closed the circle and stuck her arm up against Nickie's. "Let's power the heck out of this thing."

That seemed to fix the issue, and the transport bubble bloomed, detaching from Nickie's black ring to hover there in front of the witches at a size big enough to fit all three of them. Right before the ensorcelled witches and wizards of Circle C Ranch reached them in a random neighbor's yard, the Hadstrom sisters stepped into the transport bubble and disappeared.

CHAPTER TEN

The transport bubble burst and left all three Hadstrom sisters in the dark.

"Okay, what—ah!" Nickie batted at the cold, damp, hairy-feeling tendrils of something brushing across her face and neck and shoulders.

"Who wasn't thinking about the energy core?" Laura shouted.

"You sure it wasn't *you,* Dr. Let's Follow the Trees?" Emily spat out a mouthful of dirt and fibrous something, then blinked against the dark and the slowly brightening blue light all around them. "But this looks a lot like a bunch of tree roots dangling through a giant hole in the ground.

"What?" Laura stopped struggling against the creepily tail-like things catching in her hair and took a minute to look at them. "You're totally right, Em."

"Yeah, I know."

All the dangling roots pulsed with an even brighter blue light, then the light shot down the network of roots. The tunnel lit up in a wave away from the Hadstrom sisters, and by the time the illuminated tree roots disappeared into darkness again, another blue light started at the witches and repeated the process.

"Huh." Emily brushed more thin roots aside with her forearm. "I guess this really does qualify as still following the trees."

"And now you believe me, don't you?" Laura laughed and pulled the dangling roots aside to move forward down the tunnel. "If the trees hadn't grown all the way through the ceiling down here, this would look exactly like all the other passages around the other chambers. I'm willing to bet that last energy core is at the end of the lights."

They slowly headed down the tunnel, their speed hampered by the thick curtains of roots they constantly had to move aside in order to take a few steps forward. Half of the roots had grown all the way through the tunnel from top to bottom and wouldn't budge.

"See, *this* makes a lot more sense." Emily had to walk in a wide circle around a particularly large root that might as well have been a tree down here. "This escape pod has been down here since right after the ship set off on the first voyage. Billions of years, right? Why is *this* chamber the only one overgrown with a bunch of roots?"

"Maybe it's the neighborhood," Nickie offered.

"Hey, look." Laura pointed up ahead at a point in the curving passageway where the flashing lights running across the roots took a sharp left turn before winking out. "Almost there."

"It's never taken us this long before."

"Everything takes a lot more time now, Em. No magic, no instant results."

When they finally reached the end of the pulsing roots, the sisters were blocked off by a thick wall of vines and roots and whatever else was growing down here.

"Great." Emily sighed and pulled a net of tiny, hair-like roots off her shoulder. "Open Sesame?"

"Have you ever seen that work?" Nickie asked.

"Worth a shot when nothing works the way it's supposed to, huh? Hey, Laura. Turn around and take, like… two steps back."

"For what?"

Emily waved her sister back away from the wall of roots and vines. "So I can open your fancy backpack and grab our potions. Remember those?"

"Oh. Sure." Laura clung to the vines dangling on either side of her and lifted her boots high over all the gnarled tree roots protruding from the passage floor.

Emily unzipped the pack, pulled out the padded and potion-filled lockbox, and steadied it on one arm while she flipped up the latches. Nickie shifted closer through the curtain of roots to hold the box for her instead. "Hey, thanks. Okay. So first, we need to get into that chamber."

"Yep. That's pretty much the first step for everything. Get there." Laura heard the little pop of a vial being unstoppered and she glanced at Emily over her shoulder. "What are you doing?"

"Getting us inside." Emily spread her arms, the open vial of bright orange potion in one hand and the cork in the other. "Unless you brought a magically sharpened machete or something."

"Wait a minute. No, Em." Laura twisted around toward her sister. Her boot caught under one of the upturned roots, and she lost her balance. The dangling vines around her shivered a little and flashed a pale blue. The oldest Hadstrom sister blinked and found herself suspended by dangling roots without ever really having fallen closer to the ground at all. "Woah. Did they…"

"You're definitely caught in a bunch of tree roots." Nickie frowned over the lid of the open lockbox. "I honestly can't tell if that's luck, or because the trees actually moved to catch you."

"Emily." Laura got her feet back under her and stood. "You can't blow up a bunch of trees underground."

"Why not?"

"Because they're…they helped us *get* here." Laura nodded at the open vial. "Close that thing right now."

"Hey, it's not like I want to hurt anything, but if we need to get in there, we need to get in there. Unless you wanna try to have a conversation with a bunch of roots, right?" Emily stared at the wall of roots blocking them from the chamber. "I'm pretty sure we're not gonna get anywhere by staring at them and saying, 'Hey, there, trees. Please move aside. We'd like to blow up the last energy core and start putting magic back together so Austin doesn't rip itself apart.'"

Nickie stared at the overgrown roots blocking them from the chamber. "I mean, it's a start."

"Yeah, right." Emily rolled her eyes and laughed. "Since when is that—holy trees! They're moving."

The overgrown passageway filled with the muted echo of all the glowing blue vines and tree roots scraping across each other, pulling away and retracting into the earthen walls. And then the entrance into the energy-core chamber was clear.

Laura let out a short, amused hum. "Yeah, Em. Looks like that's a lot better than blowing everything up. Good work."

Nickie gave her little sister a nod of approval and stepped past Emily to follow Laura into the chamber.

"Wow." Emily gave the retracted roots a hesitant glance and slowly settled the cork back into the vial of explosive potion. "Definitely wasn't expecting that."

The energy core in this chamber looked like all the others—the clear, glass-like cylinder in the center, held in place by the metal cradle in the floor and the matching attachment in the ceiling. But the rest of the chamber wasn't quite the same as the other eleven the Hadstrom sisters had entered in the last few weeks.

"This is different." Nickie cocked her head and stared at the row of panels along the right-hand wall of the chamber. "Looks kinda like that Kashgar watchtower under Barton Creek, right, Em?"

"Kinda, yeah." Emily's mouth dropped open, and she pointed to the mechanism centered in the control panels, which were all dark and dusty and in no way operative. "Except the watchtower was missing one of those. Anybody else think that little doohickey looks an awful lot like a giant metal steering wheel?"

"The kind on an old airplane, maybe." Laura walked down the row of control panels, studying the engraved symbols she couldn't read and all manner of buttons and levers she didn't recognize. "I think it's called a yoke."

"Whatever it's called," Nickie added, "I think we walked

into the control center of the escape pod. Like, to drive the thing."

"It's called a bridge." When Emily caught the blank stares from each of her sisters, she shrugged. "What?"

"Are you studying old instruction manuals for Velikan escape pods in your spare time, Em?" Laura swept up a thick layer of dust from the closest panel, then wiped it off on her shorts.

"No…" The youngest Hadstrom sister frowned in confusion. "But it's called a bridge in like, every sci-fi movie ever. Seriously, I'm kinda baffled that didn't click for either of you."

"Well, we're not in a sci-fi movie." Laura headed across the chamber toward the energy core. "But, I think Nickie's right about this chamber. No wonder the trees were acting so weird."

Nickie readjusted the lockbox full of potion vials in her arms and turned to look back through the entrance into the passageway beyond. The tree roots still pulsed with blue light around the entrance, but they hadn't moved back into place to block the witches' escape. "And the roots growing down here to keep people out. Anyone who isn't us, I guess."

"I wonder how long they've been here," Emily added. "Like, did the trees start trying to block this chamber off because of the Gorafrex, or were they already here?"

"I don't think it matters, Em." Laura nodded at the explosive potion in her sister's hand and moved a few steps away from the energy core. "The most important thing is that we destroy this last energy core. After that, we have a guarantee that magic won't get any worse."

"Like that's even possible." With a wry laugh, Emily glanced at the vial and decided to leave it stoppered. "But we get to work on fixing it. Ready?"

"Go for it."

They all took another few steps back, then Emily chucked the vial as hard as she could at the energy core. The glass shattered against the clear column, spilling orange potion all over the glass-like material and the stone floor.

Emily eyed the puddle of potion and the red streaks dripping down the side of the energy core, the silence in the chamber punctured by the steady, echoing drip.

"Nickie?"

"Yeah."

"I thought you said Emily's potions always work."

At the same time, Emily and Nickie both said, "They do."

Emily shook her head. "I don't get it. This is *definitely* an explosive—"

A massive crack split the air, followed by a burst of bright orange light shooting across the floor and all the way up the energy core. The ground shuddered beneath them, and the soft, ominous creak of glass splintering with thousands of fractures followed.

The sisters ducked away from the second orange explosion and the few shattered pieces of energy-core column flying across the room. Something creaked and groaned around them, but there wasn't much more than that.

"That can't be it." Emily brushed a thick piece of glass-like material off her shoulder. "What happened to the blue and green sparks? The big explosions? The whole thing… you know. Falling over?"

"Yeah, it doesn't really look all that destroyed, does it?" Staring at the energy core, Nickie opened the lockbox again and sidled toward Emily. "Wanna try again?"

Emily stared at Nickie and hesitantly reached for another orange potion nestled in the foam cushioning. She paused. "I'm waiting for one of you to tell me this is a bad idea."

"Really?" Laura hummed in surprise. "Well, I appreciate your sudden restraint, Em. But, this might be the only time both of us are telling you to keep blowing stuff up until we finish this."

"Wow. This day is so weird." Emily shrugged and finally grabbed the next explosive vial. "But, I'm not gonna question it. How about a little sister-magic backup this time?"

"Yep." Laura set a hand on Emily's shoulder, and once Nickie had closed the lockbox and tucked it under her arm, she did the same. "Ready when you are."

"Awesome." Grinning, Emily drew back her arm and hurled the second vial at the energy core. All three Hadstrom legacy rings flashed at once—copper, silver, and black. The vial burst from Emily's hand and almost disappeared with how quickly it shot forward.

They didn't even have enough time to hear the vial shatter. The next second, the entire energy core erupted with blue and green sparks and a burst of orange light. The first explosive wave knocked all three witches off their feet and tossed them across the chamber. The second wave came a split-second later while the Hadstrom sisters were still flying backward through the air.

The trees that had twisted themselves into a protective wall around the last standing energy-core chamber moved more quickly than they had in centuries. Pulsing blue roots shot out from the entrance into the passageway beyond and curled themselves around legs, arms, and torsos.

Emily saw nothing but fiery orange and electric-blue light, then everything went cold and dark. Her stomach lurched, and something soft and cold and thick shuddered around her entire body. She tried to call out for her sisters, but her open mouth quickly filled with a thick, dry, crumbly substance that made her cough. *Great. Wish someone had told me that dying tastes like overcooked, unflavored potatoes.*

CHAPTER ELEVEN

The empty, overgrown lot in the Circle C Ranch neighborhood pulsed with bright blue light. The tall weeds shivered and rustled, then the undisturbed earth erupted in a shower of dark soil and roots and pebbles. Dry grasses and ripped plants were tossed in every direction, followed by three witches with dark hair.

The Hadstrom sisters landed in the tall weeds of the empty lot. The ground shuddered again, and a few whipping tendrils of pulsing blue roots lashed around the outside of the massive hole before disappearing into it completely. Then the neighborhood fell back into its normal, silent peace under the noonday sun, and the pulsing blue light streaking through the trees on Bexley Lane faded away.

"Ow..." Nickie groaned and rolled over onto her back in the grass. Rubbing her side, she glared at the closed lockbox she'd fallen on top of and drew in a sharp, hissing breath. "What happened?"

Emily spat out a mouthful of damp soil and coughed a

few times. Then she tried rubbing the rest of the dirt off her tongue with the hem of her t-shirt. "Dirt. Oh, man. It's *dirt*."

"You guys okay?" Laura cradled her head and pushed herself up until she sat with her head barely a few inches over the tops of the weeds she hadn't flattened when she'd landed.

"I think so." Nickie grimaced. "Wouldn't be surprised if I broke something, though."

"We're not dead!" Emily threw her head back and cackled.

Her older sisters shot each other a wary glance. Laura blinked heavily and rubbed her pounding temples. "I don't think it would hurt this much if we were, Em."

"I totally thought—" Another fit of laughter overwhelmed the youngest Hadstrom sister, and she fell over into the weeds again.

"I'm really glad you're enjoying this so much," Nickie muttered. "Good job with the explosions."

"Yeah, that second one was…" A wave of dizziness washed over Laura, and she forced herself through it. "Did you make both of those potions in the same batch, Em?"

With another long, drawn-out sigh and a few more chuckles, Emily flopped her arms down onto the ground beside her and stared at the cloudless blue sky. "Um… no, actually. One of them was left over from what I made right before Nickie and I came to rescue you."

"I'm guessing the second vial was from what you made today," Nickie muttered.

"Huh. That's so *cool*."

"Which part, Em?" Laura pulled an uprooted dandelion

—yellow flower, long stem, spiny leaves, and the entire root system—from her hair and tossed it aside. "The part where you made two different strengths of explosion, or the part where using two different explosive potions almost killed us?"

"That it took less than forty-eight hours for that first batch to go from a pile of TNT to one of those sparkler fireworks." Emily barked out another laugh. "I'll have to make them fresh every time we go out to blow a few things up. Battle the Gorafrex, maybe. Create some diversions for—"

"I think you're getting a little ahead of yourself." Nickie slowly pushed herself to her feet and pressed her hand against the sharp pain in her ribs. "But now we have zero energy cores left to destroy. One more point for team Hadstrom, right?"

"It almost wasn't." Laura turned over her shoulder and gazed at the trees in the well-maintained yard beside the empty plot. The blue lights were completely gone now, and the trees no longer moved. "I have a whole new appreciation for the trees around here, though."

"Like the 'let's go hug some trees' kind, or the 'walk by with a silent nod' kind?" Emily stood, swayed a little on her feet, and held out both her arms to steady herself.

"General appreciation, Em." Laura took her youngest sister's offered hand and gratefully accepted the help in getting up off the ground. "A simple please worked pretty well when we wanted to get inside the chamber. Even through your sarcasm."

"I know, right? That was trippy."

Laura ignored Emily's bafflement. "I think a simple thank you will be enough for the trees."

Emily threw her arms out wide and spun around in a circle, shouting, "Thank you, trees!"

Nickie burst out laughing but stopped with a wince and clutched her ribs again.

"You okay?" Laura frowned and stepped toward her sister.

"Yeah. I'm good. A little bruised, probably." Nickie lifted the bottom of her loose maroon tank top to peer at her ribs. "Or at least, they will be tomorrow. I'm a little sore."

"Okay." Laura nodded and watched her sister pick the lockbox up out of the weeds. "If it gets worse, though, let me know."

"Why wouldn't I?"

Emily dusted off her jeans and pointed at Nickie. "You didn't tell us about hearing the Gorafrex drums for a long time until you almost passed out."

"Well, a few sore ribs don't really have anything to do with the Gorafrex, Em."

"Hey." Laura raised her eyebrows at Nickie and dipped her head. "Promise me you won't ignore it and try to sleep it off if it gets worse, okay?"

"Laura, I'm fine. We all got tossed out of that giant hole by some quick-thinking tree roots. But sure, I promise. Ready to get outta here?"

"Oh, yeah…" Emily turned around slowly and scanned the neighborhood streets on both sides of the empty lot, which were once again empty. "We should definitely get a move on before the Gorafrex starts banging on the Clubhouse walls with that drumbeat again. I don't even wanna think about what might happen if that thing gets out around all the witches and wizards in this neighborhood. Hey, you think that's a thing?"

"We went over this, Em. I have no idea if there's enough magic in the Clubhouse—"

"No, I mean like this neighborhood. You think all these magicals moved in here together on purpose, like a witch-and-wizard community neighborhood kinda thing?"

Nickie chuckled and sucked in a sharp breath, trying to ignore the pain in her ribs. "That makes it sound more like a cult."

"Huh."

"That's an interesting idea, though, Em." Laura swept her hair away from her face, peeling a few strands already sticking to her neck in the muggy heat of midday. "Remember when we first found out about the energy cores all over the place under Austin?"

The sisters picked their way through the overgrown weeds and stepped out onto the sidewalk before heading back down Beachmont Lane toward Nickie's car.

"You mean the blood map on that witch's wall?"

"Uh...no, Em." Laura blinked and stared down the street. "That's something I wouldn't mind forgetting completely. I'm talking about what Nathan said about this ship working with its own intentions, even when it comes to a massive Velikan escape pod built around the Gorafrex in an iron prison."

"The ship definitely has its own intentions." Nickie tucked the lockbox under her other arm to keep it away from her sore ribs. "I bet our arboreal rescuers had a lot to do with that, too."

"That's what I mean," Laura continued. "I thought it was so weird that there would be a bunch of energy cores *under* really populated places like they are. Or were, I guess."

"Oh." Emily nodded. "Like under the Thinkery and the airport."

"Yeah, and a few other neighborhoods, too. I mean, I don't know how many magicals were living in those other places, but the point is, Nathan told me something about how civilizations on this ship were drawn to specific places for a reason. Obviously, the energy core under the airport wasn't put there centuries ago with the intention of someday having an airport right on top of it."

"He said that places like the Thinkery and the airport were built where are they *because of* the energy cores, right?"

Laura glanced at Nickie and nodded. "Yeah. Hey, you can stick that box back in my pack, if you—"

"I'm fine, Laura. I can carry a box full of potions for another block."

"Wait a minute." Emily stepped up between her sisters on the sidewalk and frowned at Laura. "Are you saying the witches and wizards all moved to this neighborhood because the energy core is right under it?"

"Maybe not all of them, Em. But at least the ones on this street, yeah." Laura shrugged and studied the overhanging branches of the live oak in the next yard, its sprawling shadow giving the sisters a moment of shady relief from the sun, if not from the humid heat. "Think about it, though. Dad kinda said the same thing to us when we finally had that family-legacy talk."

"Yeah, one day too late." Emily snorted, but her smile

faded when Laura shot her an unamused look. "I know. Too soon. Sorry. Dad said what, now?"

"That our family's been living in Austin since the very first Hadstrom witches who locked the Gorafrex up in the first place. Granted, we have a responsibility as guardians of that prison, and it's always passed down through the family. But, none of us have ever moved away from Austin. He said we can't."

"Doesn't Dad's Aunt Tabitha live in Rocksprings, though?" Nickie asked.

"Yeah, but Grandpa was one of five kids. Only three rings." Emily stuck up her thumb and eyed her copper legacy ring.

"Yep. I bet that Great-Aunt Tabitha was one of those two kids who *didn't* get a ring."

"Talk about an ego blow, right?" Emily scratched the side of her head and glanced down at the spray of dirt that fell out of her hair.

"Or, she moved away from Austin once the rings passed on to Dad, Uncle Mark, and Aunt Julie," Laura continued.

"I don't know…" They reached the car parked at the curb on the corner, and Nickie walked behind it to open the trunk. "I still don't see how the Hadstrom legacy and being prison guardians explains the way this city was built right on top of a giant escape pod that could have easily wiped all of Austin completely off the map. And taken this whole ship with it, probably."

"Right, but it *didn't*."

When Nickie set the lockbox in the trunk and shut it again, she found Emily standing beside the car, grinning at her.

"We destroyed all the working parts of that escape pod, and now there aren't any energy cores left. So, Austin's safe."

"Almost safe, Em." Nickie moved around the car and opened the driver's side door as her sisters climbed into the car. "We still have to get the Gorafrex out of the Clubhouse and back into the prison."

Laura shut her door and buckled her seatbelt in the passenger seat. "But now that the energy cores are out of the picture, magic can start fixing itself. When that's done, everything's gonna be a lot easier for us."

"And for the Gorafrex." Nickie started the engine.

"Oh, come on, Nickie." Emily leaned forward in the back seat and patted the side of her sister's seat. "Three Hadstroms put that thing away in the first place. And if you think about it, we have a bunch of stuff that they *didn't*."

"Oh, yeah?" Laura pressed her lips together and looked over her shoulder at Emily. "What's that?"

Emily thumped back against the back seat and grinned, counting off on her fingers. "The knowledge that three Hadstroms actually *can* put that thing away, for starters. Plus, whatever clues and wisdom our family might have passed down. Potions. The Hadstrom-sister jumper cables. And, most importantly, two weeks of fighting the Gorafrex, saving the Peabrains it used, and still somehow keeping our lives together all after magic booked itself a one-way trip to crazy town."

Laura and Nickie both chuckled as Nickie drove them out of the Circle C Ranch neighborhood and back toward the highway.

"That doesn't exactly make us sound like we know what we're doing, Em."

The youngest Hadstrom sister glanced up into the rearview mirror and caught Nickie's gaze in the reflection. "Are you kidding me? Compared to the original Hadstroms, we're basically seasoned vets."

CHAPTER TWELVE

They pulled up in front of their house on Pressler Street a few minutes before 1:00 p.m. Emily slammed the back door shut and bounded up the stairs to the top of the hill.

"Gotta hit the shower," she called over her shoulder. "Whoever else wants one has to wait."

Nickie pulled the lockbox of potions out of her trunk, then she and Laura headed a lot more patiently toward their house. "At least now she's in a better mood."

"I mean, there's a fine line between Emily in a better mood and Emily being in a rush." Laura shrugged as she stepped through the door and waited for her sister to enter before shutting it. "But, I think you're right. Even if she got this shift to pick up for the one she missed, I'm pretty sure she's looking forward to it."

They headed into the dining room. Both the padded box of potions and Laura's trekking pack joined Emily's array of potion-making materials. Nickie smirked when the sound of Emily's loud, seriously off-key singing rose over the echo of the running shower. "You think we can convince her to make something for lunch before she heads off to make everyone else's dinner?"

"Not unless you already wanted a bowl of cereal." When they stepped into the kitchen, Laura grabbed the last banana from the fruit bowl. "Or a banana. Want this one?"

"How 'bout we split the banana *and* what's left from breakfast?"

"Deal."

The older Hadstrom sisters made quick work of heating up the leftover frittata, then they sat at the kitchen table and made the most of their lunch. "Hey, you think those trees know who we are?"

Laura pressed her lips down around her mouthful of food and put all her focus into chewing and swallowing first. "You know, before everything that happened this morning, I would've written that question off as you being you."

Nickie laughed. "What's that supposed to mean?"

"Come on. You're a professional musician dating your manager—"

"Correction." Nickie held up a finger. "With my boyfriend as my manager. Chuck and I were already together when he started his business. And what does that have to do with the trees, exactly?"

Laura shook her head and took a few gulps of water. "I was gonna finish that list with something about how your music is your magic and that you were literally dancing around the park barefoot and playing your guitar the day we met the Tree Folk for the first time."

"Uh-huh." With a coy smile, Nickie pointed her fork at

her big sister. "So, you're trying to say I'm a big hippie who *almost* signed a record deal, so asking if the trees know who we are falls neatly in line with that definition."

"Well, I wasn't gonna bring up the record deal thing, but kinda."

"Okay..." Nickie finally let herself laugh a little and shook her head as she returned her focus to her microwaved frittata. "So we're clear, you're the one eating half a banana with a fork."

"Because *you* took the end with the peel!" Laura stuck the last piece of banana in her mouth and whisked the fork away with an exaggerated tug. "My point is that, after that last energy core, yeah. I think the trees *do* know who we are. Even if they only started blocking off the energy core after the Gorafrex escaped and after magic started to fall apart, they still wouldn't have moved out of the way for anyone else."

"*Especially* if they were trying to keep the Gorafrex out of there, too." Nickie laughed again and sat back in her chair. "Or maybe we've gone as crazy as magic, huh? Talking about trees knowing things and trying to protect the last energy core from a witch-killing creature that doesn't even have a body."

"It's part of the whole ship trying to protect itself. I mean, sure, it would've saved us one massive headache if the trees had decided to do something *before* I accidentally set the Gorafrex free."

"I don't think that's how it works, Laura. Not that I know how this entire ship works or even how that prison's supposed to hold the Gorafrex for centuries without anybody noticing."

"I know." Laura's fork clattered softly onto her empty plate. "It wouldn't surprise me if the trees or anything else at the Greenbelt didn't try to stop me from poking around the prison *because* they knew who I was."

"Yeah, why try to stop a Hadstrom witch from handling the responsibility that's been passed down through every generation of Hadstroms since the beginning, right?" Nickie shoveled her last bite into her mouth. "At least we have proof that trees can't read minds."

"Very funny."

"None of that matters now, though." Nickie ran a hand through her hair, then clasped her hands behind her back for a nice shoulder stretch. "We've done everything we needed to do to make things right again. It took a little longer than we wanted—ow."

She drew in a sharp breath and released her stretch to rub her sore ribs.

"That doesn't sound good." Laura got up from the table and grabbed both of their plates. "Didn't Emily say she made some healing potions?"

"I don't need healing potions." Nickie wrinkled her nose, rubbed her tender ribs a little, then pushed herself to her feet. "Besides, I'm the one with the super awesome healing magic, remember? I think Emily also said *that,* too."

"Then maybe you wanna try some of that super awesome healing magic on yourself." After sticking the dishes in the sink, Laura turned around and leaned back against the counter. "Hey, I've been banged up a lot, too."

"Oh, really?" Nickie raised an eyebrow.

"I'm talking about when I'm out in the field. Rockslides are a lot more common than I'd like to admit. Dead trees fall over. Caves that look a lot sturdier end up…not being that sturdy. But I always make sure I have *something* with me, in case I hurt myself a lot more than I expected."

"Like Advil and a couple of Ace bandages?"

Laura rolled her eyes. Above them, Emily's quick, urgent footsteps moved down the hall and thumped down the stairs.

"Seriously, I'm *fine*. Just landed the wrong way on a metal box. Emily almost swallowed a mouthful of dirt, and you're not breathing down her neck to make sure she brushes her teeth or anything—"

"And I *did* brush my teeth, by the way." Emily quickly moved through the dining room into the kitchen and shot both of her sisters a confused frown. "The real question is why you guys are talking about my hygiene."

"Nickie doesn't want to use your healing potions, Em."

"That's not it."

"You can if you think you need it." Emily passed her sisters and headed for the counter. "Those are the purple ones in the box. But, now that we killed the last energy core, magic should be coming back online any minute now. So, you can heal yourself, and—hey. I thought we still had one banana."

Laura smirked. "It was delicious."

"Glad you enjoyed it. Oh. We still have some frittata left from breakfast."

Nickie stopped her sister before Emily got to the fridge. "Not anymore."

Emily turned around and glanced between her sisters. "You microwaved it, didn't you?"

Laura and Nickie shrugged at the same time.

"I'm seriously *this close* to throwing that microwave in the trash. You guys realize that it kills eighty percent of the flavor of just about everything, right?"

"Yeah, Em." Laura folded her arms. "I think you've told us a few dozen times."

Nickie chuckled. "Hey, we can't all be gourmet chefs and magically whip up an awesome meal out of all the random stuff left in the fridge."

"It was pretty magical, wasn't it?" With a small smile, Emily opened the fridge, peered inside, then quickly closed it again. "You know what you *can* do, though?"

"Go grocery shopping? That was already on my list."

The youngest Hadstrom sister spun around and shot Nickie a thumbs-up. "*And* you can read minds. How cool is that? Thanks, Nickie. Leave the receipt out, and I'll pitch in for food when I get home tonight."

"No problem."

Laura opened the pantry above the coffee maker. "Em, I think we have some crackers or something if you still need some food—"

"Nope. I killed those last night." Emily's keys jingled in her hand as she headed toward the foyer. "I get a shift meal. Might even get to eat it. Wish me luck!"

"Good luck."

"You won't need it," Laura called after her.

"Thanks!" Emily stuck out her thumb without turning back, and then she was out the door and headed to her first full evening shift at Meadowlark Tavern.

"She's not gonna have any time to eat through their Friday dinner rush," Nickie muttered.

"She better make time." Laura downed the rest of her

water and set the glass in the sink with the dirty plates. "The only thing worse than Emily on an empty stomach is Emily on zero sleep."

"At least she had that."

Laura bent over the trashcan and found two empty boxes of crackers. "Not if she stayed up to eat all the crackers in the house."

"Well, we can go buy more. You wanna come to the store with me?"

"Actually..." Laura met her sister's gaze and forced a smile that made Nickie instantly suspicious. "I was planning on doing something else."

"Okay, this is the part where I tell you that you look like you're hiding something."

"I'm not hiding anything. I'm gonna go talk to Mom."

Nickie folded her arms and narrowed her eyes. "Mom's at work."

"She has Fridays off this month. I checked." Laura skirted past her sister and headed through the mudroom into the living room.

"Laura?"

"Why is me meeting up with Mom suddenly such a weird thing that you have to ask a bunch of questions?"

Nickie followed her big sister into the living room and watched Laura double-checking everything in her purse. "Because *you're* acting weird about it. That's really the only red flag I need."

With a sigh, Laura stopped rifling through her purse and slung it over her shoulder. "Okay, fine. I want to talk to Mom about that guy you and Emily met."

"What guy?"

"You know, the guy who used to be her teacher or whatever."

"The *soothsayer?*"

"Yeah. You guys got to go meet him and hear a bunch of stuff about wards so powerful that they've been banned from all magical use everywhere." When Nickie's eyes widened, Laura laughed and headed toward the door. "Relax. I'm not gonna try to learn banned magic or anything. Does that even sound like me?"

"Not normally. But when regular magic doesn't work, you're the perfect person to go looking for what *does* work. Maybe not with Astro, though. That dude was creepy."

"Creepy doesn't bother me. And I'm not using banned magic, okay? Even when magic comes back like it's supposed to with no more energy cores." Laura opened the front door and paused to shoot her sister a reassuring smile. "But if Astro knew how to disassemble the wards the Gorafrex put in the park when you guys found me, that's *exactly* who I want to go talk to next. Mom can show me where to find him."

"Shut up in his smoky house, probably."

"And, who knows? Maybe he'll *see* something about how to put the Gorafrex back in that prison without having to fight it again. Then we can finally be done with this whole thing. So…lemme know how much I owe you for groceries, okay?"

"Yeah, but—"

Laura shut the door, and Nickie puffed out a dejected sigh through loose lips.

"Awesome. Whole house to myself." She leaned back against the wall between the living room and the foyer, and a muffled snort made her turn. Speed lay curled up on the couch, his chin resting on his paws as he stared at her with drooping eyes. "Okay, not completely to myself. At least you're here, buddy."

Nickie went to the couch and plopped down next to their immortal family pet. The minute she reached out to scratch behind his ears, Speed crawled across the cushion on his belly to get closer. "How you holdin' up after your epic fight with our Hadstrom-family enemy, huh?"

Speed snorted and flopped over onto his back.

"Yeah, looks like you don't have any problem recovering." Nickie rubbed his belly, and the dog stretched out his front paws to give her more room. One of them scraped against the young witch's ribs, and she sucked in a sharp breath. "Jeeze. I hope I don't have any problems recovering, either."

She lifted the bottom of her shirt again to look at her side. That might have been the beginning of a bruise she saw there, but it wasn't anything noticeable or alarming. With a deep breath, Nickie focused on the healing magic she'd been using a lot more recently until magic had lost its ability to do much of anything. *So, let's get to healing up this super annoying bruise.*

The black legacy ring on her thumb sputtered with a dark light, but that was it. No electric pulse of magic through her. No purple healing bubbles coming from her mouth or fingertips or even the ring itself.

Nickie leaned back against the couch and picked up right where she'd left off with rubbing Speed's upturned belly. "It took a few days for magic to stop working, so maybe it'll take a few days to completely come back again.

Well, I have no problem waiting. And I don't really have anything better to do right now."

Speed's mouth popped open, his tongue lolled out over his drooping upper lip, and Nickie didn't have any warning whatsoever before the immortal dog's stink hit her nose. "Oh, come on, buddy. I need to find something better to do."

CHAPTER THIRTEEN

Prepping for the dinner rush and manning her station in Meadowlark Tavern's kitchen had given Emily plenty of experience already. But, cooking for a few orders and getting caught up in the first hour and a half of the dinner rush, at most, wasn't anywhere close to what she'd taken on tonight. A brief glance at the clock over the swinging door into the dining room told her it was almost 6:15 p.m.

Seriously? Emily blinked, finished drizzling the truffle glaze over the plated salmon in front of her, and set the plate up on the line. *I don't know if I can keep doing this for much longer.*

When she looked up at the next ticket, her gaze settled on John's face instead. He stood on the other side of the line, sweat dripping down the side of his neck and under the collar of the white button-up shirt of his server's uniform. He shot her a grateful smile, and Emily stabbed the old ticket before moving onto the next.

"You okay?" John muttered.

"Yep. Just gotta keep my head in the—"

"Eighty-six Brussels sprouts," Chef Gaulsten called.

"Seriously?" Chef Ansler stormed across the kitchen to mutter something fierce and very serious to his closest chef. "I *knew* we should've doubled the order."

"You seem tense." John gave Emily a half-smile and quickly arranged his table's five dinner plates on the serving tray. "You sure everything's fine?"

Besides Emily, the chef at the stove whose name she couldn't even dredge up right now tossed a pan over the burner. Oil splashed and vegetables turned over and the fire lighting the burning flared up in a bright, hot flash. "Yep. I need to focus. You should take that to your table."

"Let's go, let's go!" Chef Ansler clapped his hands and pointed at the door. "Get that tray off the line and keep moving. Come on!"

John bent his knees to settle the tray on his shoulder, then stood and quickly disappeared into the dining room.

"Feel free to shout that out, too, Hadstrom." Chef Ansler pointed at Emily but didn't look at her as he walked past the line to check on someone else's station. "Bottom line is to keep the plates moving. Hurt his feelings if you must. He'll get over it."

"Yes, Chef." Emily's cheeks flushed hot as she waited for the next ordered plate to reach her at the end of the station so she could drizzle another piece of salmon or garnish another quail or slather sauce and dried herbs onto the next pork shoulder. *Hurting his feelings is the last thing I wanna do.*

Flames from the stove on the other side of her flared up

this time. Someone behind her dropped a pot, cursed, and kicked it out of the way before grabbing another.

"Why is this ticket still up here?"

"Where's the braised asparagus?"

"I need more goat cheese!"

The door swung open again, and a server whose name Emily thought was Charlotte barreled back into the kitchen with wide eyes, a fully untouched plate in her hands. "Table fourteen wants a redo on the salmon."

Emily didn't realize the server was talking to her until the other woman stopped on the other side of the line and set the plate down. "What's wrong with the salmon?"

"Said it's not cooked enough."

"Hey, hey. What's this?" Chef Ansler stormed toward them and bent his head toward the returned plate. "What's wrong with that salmon?"

"Not cooked enough."

"How'd they order it?"

"Medium."

"And that idiot wants it *more* cooked? Might as well just burn it to a crisp and call it good." Ansler slapped his hand down on the stainless-steel line. "Go tell Garder."

Charlotte hurried off to talk to the chef manning the grill and all the salmon. Emily stared at the plates stalling in a quickly growing line at her station. Chef Ansler yelled something completely incomprehensible at Garder on the grill, and Emily tuned it out. *Focus. On the food. Garnish and sauce. That's it.*

"Order up!"

"There's nothing wrong with the salmon!"

"Where's the summer ravioli?"

Emily's hand knocked against the small dish of rosemary in front of her, and she tossed way more onto the quail in front of her than she wanted. Gritting her teeth, she quickly pulled most of it off and wiped the edge of the plate with her apron.

"Does nobody in the kitchen know how to fill a damn bottle of—"

Emily blinked and struck the bell for the next order up before turning to the next one.

John came rushing back into the kitchen and stared at whatever fit Chef Ansler was throwing in the corner of the kitchen now. "What's up with him?"

"I don't know."

"Hey, do you have the dinner salad that's supposed to go with this?" John pointed at the plate in front of him, then glanced around the kitchen.

"Crap. No. No, I don't—" Emily drew a deep breath, her face still hot and her ears ringing now with the chaos. "House salad for twenty-two! Where is it?"

"What?" Ansler pointed at her and screamed, "Get Hadstrom her house salad two minutes ago!"

Emily shook her head and checked the next ticket. *He really doesn't need to call me out like that. I can handle it.*

"Here, here. Salad."

She didn't even look up at the other station chef quickly dropping the salad off on the line next to John.

"Thanks." He picked up both plates but didn't rush out immediately. "Hey, you sure you're okay? You're kinda—"

"I'm fine!" She looked up from the rice and filleted red snapper and only had a split second to take in his startled expression before she apparently couldn't stop herself. "I need this space for the next order. Take that out."

"Huh." John blinked and turned quickly away from her before passing back through the swinging door.

That's not what I wanted to say. What's wrong with me? She frowned in concentration and finished the rest of the garnish. The plate slid down the line and she worked quickly on the next in the same order.

"Hadstrom, you almost finished with table eight?"

"Yes, Chef."

"Keep it moving!"

Another server rushed into the kitchen and started filling up a tray with the dishes Emily was finishing. His thick glasses were half-fogged from the heat in the kitchen. "Hey."

"Hey." Emily kept working.

"This has mornay."

"Yep."

"They ordered no mornay."

The young witch huffed out a quick breath. *Keep it under control.* "If that's what they ordered, it needs to be on the ticket."

"It *is* on the ticket," the server replied. "I put it into the system."

"Obviously not." Emily's hands moved quickly over the next plates in front of her.

"Are you kidding me?"

The bin of silverware at the end of the line rattled. *Please, not now.* Emily couldn't bring herself to look up at the guy. "I made what you put in the system. Go take those out to the table. You're backing us up."

"Yeah, after you get rid of the mornay."

"How many times do I have to tell you, I—" The whole bin of silverware launched off the end of the line, scattering forks and knives and spoons in every direction across the floor.

"What the hell!" Ansler shouted.

Emily grabbed a spring of parsley and saw the copper legacy ring on her thumb sputter with a faint yellow light. *No...*

"Hadstrom, why are you backed up over there?"

"I'm not!" A puff of herbs from every garnish dish in front of her spilled over onto the line at the same time.

"Customer wanted no mornay, Chef," the server explained.

"Was it on the ticket?"

Emily tried to ignore the mess and her sputtering ring and the fact that she wanted to upturn that whole tray of food onto the server who couldn't remember what he'd typed into the POS.

"Hadstrom?"

"No, Chef! It wasn't on the ticket." The spare plates under the line rattled against each other. *Stay cool, Em.*

"This table comes in every Friday," the server shouted, "and every single time, the woman at seat three always makes sure I repeat to her that there's no—"

"Okay, you wanna see the freakin' ticket?" Emily snatched up the stabbed ticket on the top and slammed it onto the line in front of the server. "Here!"

The minute she shouted, every burner in Meadowlark Tavern's kitchen exploded in foot-high flames. The other chefs cursed and leapt back.

"It's on here..." The server picked up the ticket and looked it over.

"Hey, why don't *you* get behind the line and make it yourself, then, huh?" Emily spread her arms and glared at the server through the fog covering his thick glasses. "Maybe you can read better than I can!"

The plates stacked at the end of the line shot one at a time across the kitchen, like someone was throwing frisbees at the wall. They crashed and shattered into a quickly growing pile as more plates kept whizzing by.

The server looked away from the ticket and stared at the magically flying plates.

"Hadstrom!" Chef Ansler shouted.

"I *got it*!" The steaming-hot mornay on the plate in front of the argumentative server shot up off the bed of rice and splattered up the guy's neck and up into his hair. He shouted in surprise and probably a little pain, staggering backward away from the line.

"What the hell's going on over there?" Chef Ansler stormed toward them.

Emily looked down to see the chef's knife she'd used to dice up the last round of scallions spin sideways on the stainless-steel line until the very tip pointed at the server wiping mornay off his neck. The knife lurched forward, and she slammed her hand down on the handle to keep it from going anywhere else. The row of garnish dishes flew into the air and sailed over her head, scattering rosemary, parsley, dill, and pink Himalayan salt all over the young witch's hair and the kitchen floor around her. The dishes clattered to the floor, a few of them shattered, and Emily stared at the knife handle beneath her palm. *This is so bad.*

"All right, Chef." Chef Ansler power-walked around the line until he stood next to Emily. He smacked her arm with the back of his hand and didn't look at her. "Take ten. The first wave is almost done. I got it."

Emily jerked her hand away from the chef knife that had almost become a murder weapon and whirled away from the line toward the back of the kitchen. She stormed toward the door leading out behind the restaurant and slammed her hip against the crash bar to open it. Before she staggered all the way outside into the muggy evening air, she heard Chef Ansler a lot more clearly than she should've been able to.

"Next time you're gonna blame someone back here for making the wrong order, clean your damn glasses first, huh? 'Cause I'm looking at this ticket right now, and if you actually put in that special order, I'm as blind as Hadstrom—"

The back door clicked shut behind her, and Emily paced back and forth in front of Meadowlark Tavern's outer brick wall. She drew one deep breath after another, shaking out her hands, and stared at the asphalt moving under her kitchen shoes.

"I got this. I'm handling it. Jeeze, who am I kidding. I almost sent a *knife* at the guy!"

Her hands flew up to her hair, and if she hadn't had it all pulled back in a tight ponytail, she would've been tugging on fistfuls of it.

"Get it under control, Emily. This is what you wanted—a kitchen like this. You made exactly what was on the ticket—"

The back door opened again with a metallic clang of

the crash bar, and John stepped outside to join her, wiping off his hands with a dry rag. Emily immediately stopped pacing and thumped her back against the brick wall. "Hey."

"Hey." She stared at the asphalt.

"Got time for a little break, huh?"

With a snort, she closed her eyes and bowed her head. "Probably not. Ansler pretty much ordered me to step outside."

"Yeah, that's what I meant." John chuckled and leaned back beside her against the wall. "If there really wasn't any time, he probably would've screamed at you to keep moving. I think Marino told me a while ago that none of the chefs *take* breaks. They force each other out as a courtesy."

Emily dragged her hands down both sides of her face and groaned. "I don't need a courtesy."

"But you needed a few minutes of fresh air." He reached out and slipped his fingers through hers. "And my tables got all their food, so I figured I'd come join you. That okay?"

He gave her hand a little squeeze, and Emily pushed everything she was feeling—about the kitchen, this shift, the server with foggy glasses, even Chef Ansler and John—way back down into a dark hole somewhere in her gut. "Yeah. It's fine."

They stood there for a few seconds, then John drew a quick breath. "Is there something else going on, too?"

"What?"

"Okay, don't get me wrong. Front of the house gets super hectic, and I can only imagine the kinda crazy going down in the kitchen. But I mean outside of work." He slid closer toward her against the wall, the rough brick sticking on the back of his shirt. "Because we haven't gotten to hang out very much this week. I know we have different schedules, and you've been helping Laura out. She feeling any better?"

Emily almost burst out laughing, but she managed to contain it to a short, dry chuckle. "Yeah. I think she is."

"Good. I'm glad. So, whatever else is going on, Em, maybe I can help, you know?" John bent his head toward her and smiled. "Maybe help you take your mind off whatever it is. I kinda miss you."

She closed her eyes and drew a deep breath. *I can't keep ignoring him. Not if I want him in my life at all beyond sharing a crazy-busy kitchen.* "You working tomorrow night?"

"No, actually." John grinned. "Which I thought was weird when they posted the schedule, but I'm definitely not gonna complain about it. Are we talking about going out on a Saturday night and having a normal date like all the other people who don't work on the weekends?"

Probably not... Emily swallowed. "Define normal."

John laughed. "Okay, not *normal*. We're not normal, are we?"

"That's a serious understatement."

"Okay." He reached out and gently turned Emily's face toward him. She blinked a few times and finally met his gaze. "We'll have a not-normal date tomorrow."

Emily didn't duck away or try to stop him when he dipped his head even lower and kissed her. *I can't remember the last time this happened. Feels like forever ago.*

When he pulled back, John studied her face and tucked

some of her loose hair behind her ear. Then he licked his lips and let out an airy laugh. "I have one request, though."

She waited for him to continue and playfully rolled her eyes when he didn't say anything. "You have to tell me what it is before I either agree or throw it right back in your face."

He laughed. "No sisters, okay?"

"What?" Emily pulled her head away and feigned insult. "What kinda guy asks his girlfriend *not* to bring her sisters on a date with them?"

"Yeah, I know it's a lot to ask. We probably won't have any fun without them. Hey, if it turns out to be the worst idea ever, we'll call them and demand that they come join us. How's that?"

She narrowed her eyes and pretended to consider the proposal. "I guess I can live with that."

"Awesome." John leaned in and kissed her again, this time laughing through his nose. "We're gonna have fun."

"Probably, yeah." They both laughed, and Emily had to look away so she didn't start unloading everything she was feeling on him right then. *I just need to get through the rest of this shift first without magically stabbing anybody. Then I can worry about whether I'm gonna tell John anything about what he doesn't even remember.*

CHAPTER FOURTEEN

"I really could've driven myself, you know." Laura eyed her mom as Nancy Milton drove them down Bowman Avenue. "It's not like we live all that far away from each other."

"What?" Nancy glanced at her oldest daughter before looking back through the windshield and slowing down in front of the house in need of a good remodeling. "You don't like riding in the car with me all of a sudden?"

"Well...maybe not when you're ridiculously tense."

"Laura, I'm not tense—"

"I could hear you grinding your teeth the whole drive over here."

Nancy stopped the car at the curb, shifted into park, and sighed. "All right. Maybe I'm a little tense. But I promise it has nothing to do with you or the fact that you're sitting in my car right now."

"Uh-huh." Laura squinted at her mom and pulled her purse off the floor between her feet to set it on her lap.

"Only the fact that I asked to come with you to this guy's house."

Her mom snorted and turned off the engine. "Trust me, I'd be as…hesitant about this with or without you tonight."

The car fell silent for a few seconds, and Laura popped her lips. "Why, Mom?"

"Because I really don't want to be here." Nancy gave her daughter a strained, tight-lipped smile and pulled the keys out of the ignition. "It's pretty much that simple."

"But you know this guy. Pretty well, too, right?"

"Yes…"

"Nickie and Emily said he used to be your teacher." Laura shrugged and unbuckled her seatbelt. "Even if you haven't seen him in years, he probably hasn't changed that much."

"I know, Laura. That's the problem." Nancy opened her door and quickly got out of her Camry. She paused when she reached the sidewalk and stared at the house.

"Okay." Laura shut her door and stepped up beside her mom. "So, this is about the deal you made with him, isn't it?"

Nancy raised an eyebrow and glanced sidelong at her daughter. "How much did your sisters tell you about our little visit here last night?"

"Pretty much everything, I think." Laura glanced up at the orange-and-pink sky at the beginning of sunset. "That he wouldn't hand over the ingredients to dismantle the Tenebantur wards until you agreed to come back twice a week and…I don't know. Help out around the place."

"Did they tell you what those *ingredients* were?"

"No. Something pretty valuable, though, I'm guessing."

Nancy chuckled and headed down the walkway across the yard toward her former mentor's front door. "A hair, Laura."

"A *what?*"

"Astro doesn't just make deals. He holds ridiculously absurd grudges, demands repayment completely disproportionate to whatever's requested of him, and has this... infuriating habit of setting the bar so high that no one could ever possibly meet whatever arbitrary expectations he happens to hold at any given minute."

"Wow. You really don't like this guy, do you?"

"I don't know, Laura. The man sold gorlek feathers to a poacher. Does that sound like somebody either of us would enjoy being around?"

Laura cleared her throat, blinking furiously. "He seriously did that?"

"Must've been...thirty-one years ago, at least. Yes. One of the many moments I promised myself I'd rather die than keep being his student."

"Sounds like a lot of broken promises."

Nancy let out a dry, humorless laugh. "Astro is also one of the most gifted and experienced potionmasters on the continent. All those promises to myself ended up not being nearly as important as all the things I knew I could still learn from him."

"Did you learn what you wanted?"

The Hadstrom witches stepped up onto the soothsayer's front stoop. "Of course, I did."

Nancy rapped on the door a few times. Something clattered to the floor inside the house, followed by a scrape and thump, a muffled curse, and a round of hacking coughs Laura thought would never end. Then the doorknob squeaked as it slowly turned, and the door opened barely a crack.

"You're late." Whoever spoke on the other side of the door was completely invisible behind all the white smoke seeping out into the warm evening air.

"No, I'm not." Nancy folded her arms. "Open the door."

"Oh, now. Is that a little buyer's remorse I hear, or are you simply happy to see me?"

Laura looked away from the acrid, stinging smoke to study her mom. Nancy rolled her eyes and pushed on the door. "I'm not here to play games, old man. And you know I keep my end of every deal I make it."

There was a short scuffle, another bump, and a grunt, and then the door swung fully open into the house full of thick smoke.

"Fine." Astro's voice moved away from them, coming from somewhere up ahead and to the left. "Wouldn't kill you to *act* happy about it, Milton."

"I am one hundred percent certain that's not actually true."

Laura snorted in surprise and blinked at her mom. *This isn't even close to the Nancy Milton I know. She sounds more like Emily being told to do her chores when we were kids.*

Nancy met her daughter's gaze as they stepped inside the home of the soothsayer turned potionmaster. The smoke quickly cleared away, revealing an empty and spare but severely dusty entryway inside. Laura's mom closed the door behind her and gestured toward the first room on the left.

A giant box fan hung suspended from the ceiling, pumping the not-quite-air-conditioned air around the room Laura assumed was Astro's study. Two large armchairs took up the center of the room with a small end table situated beside only one of them. The entire back wall was a massive built-in bookshelf completely stuffed with books of every shape, size, and age. In front of the bookshelf, though, was a large marble basin with a foamy, pea-green liquid simmering inside. *How is he keeping it heated without any reliable magic?*

A relatively small desk covered in scattered papers, pens, brass knickknacks, and a heavy wooden box jutted out from the right side of the study, and Astro stood behind it, facing his Friday-night guests. But, the old man's attention was somewhere else as he rummaged through the desk's open center drawer.

"Looks like the troublemaker and the softy-healer were successful after your last visit."

"Who?" Laura frowned at her mom.

Nancy opened her mouth for a dry response, but Astro cut her off. "Successful for the rest of your spawn, at least. They didn't end up hurting themselves irreversibly in the process, did they?"

"No." Nancy Milton pressed her lips together and gazed blankly at her old mentor. "They handled themselves quite well, from what I'm told."

"Oh, what you were *told*." Astro snickered. "Well, yes. Of course. Hearsay is remarkably reliable, isn't it? So good to know you trust it more than your own senses, Milton. Why is she here?"

The potionmaster still hadn't looked up to address either of the Hadstrom witches standing in his study. But he flung a gnarled hand toward Laura before jamming it back down in the desk drawer. The other hand clung firmly to the grip of the long, smooth cane beside him.

"I'm Laura. You met my sisters—"

"I know who you are, Dr. Dig Up Old Junk. I asked why you're here."

Laura's mouth dropped open, and she found herself completely speechless. *And I thought Rutilda's manners were awful. This guy blows the Velikan's welcome out of the park.*

"She wanted to meet you," Nancy replied stoically.

"That wasn't part of our arrangement."

"Clearly."

Finally, Astro looked up at the witches standing on the other side of the armchairs and scowled. "If you're here to ask me about that damn Tenebantur again, I'll stop you now and tell you to scoot your nosey little behind right back out of my house."

Laura tilted her head and decided to press forward with this seriously prickly old soothsayer. "Don't bother. I already know plenty about the Tenebantur."

"Of course, you do. Because your *sisters* told you." Astro thumped his came against the rug beneath the junk-strewn desk and wiggled his head from side to side. "Like mother, like daughters, eh? Everybody thinks they know something because they discussed it once or twice. Maybe even used a potion to destroy one of the deadliest traps in alchemical history. Ha!"

Nancy leaned toward her daughter and muttered, "You really don't have to stay."

"I'm fine." With a nod, Laura took another step forward across the study and trailed her hand over the back of the closest armchair. "It's not more hearsay, though."

Astro scoffed and returned to digging through his drawer. Now it looked like he was trying to *look* preoccupied.

"You know, when Leonidas told me he'd tested the Tenebantur with a sharp-tongued genius, he really didn't do you justice."

The old man whipped his head up again on his frail neck and squinted at Laura, leaning slightly forward over the desk. "*What?*"

"He failed to mention your serious lack of social skills or the fact that you were on your way to becoming a spell-book packrat." Laura widened her eyes and waited for the inevitable. Astro's eyes narrowed even more until they could've been mistaken for having closed completely. *Now I got his attention.* "Who knows? Maybe when you two were still talking, you were a lot cleaner, at least. Although I doubt you were any nicer."

Beside her, Laura's mom covered her mouth with a hand to hide a tiny smile of satisfaction.

"You spoke to Leonidas." Astro blinked. "About me."

"He did most of the talking in *that* conversation, honestly. But I needed to know what we were dealing with so I could warn my sisters. Your…ingredients helped all of us."

"Bah! I don't know a Leonidas—"

"Leonidas Brightwing," Laura began, folding her arms.

"Fairy. At least a few hundred years older than you, if I had to guess, but in a lot better shape. Studied with you under Hectus until after the first and only use of the Tenebantur. Before it was cast against my sisters, obviously. And the owner of Brightwing Emporium on Red River Street. He was quite helpful. He said that if anyone had more of the kind of information I needed, it would be you."

Nancy slowly turned her head to shoot her daughter a wide-eyed, surprised gaze. Laura kept staring down the crotchety old soothsayer who didn't want to take any responsibility beyond how uncomfortable he could make someone else. *And I just turned the tables on him.*

"Hmm." Astro coughed, shook his head, and started rummaging through the drawer again. But, he gave up on that attempt after only a few seconds and smacked his wrinkled lips. "Oh. *That* Leonidas."

"Yeah, and how cool is it that the owner of that apothecary—who happened to be the *other* magical the Gorafrex kidnapped, by the way—used to be such a close colleague of the soothsayer and potionmaster who took my mom as a mentee for so many years?" Laura glanced sidelong at her mom and smirked. "It kinda feels like you and I were meant to meet each other, doesn't it? I can't help thinking that we'd be complete idiots if we didn't agree to put up with each other long enough for me to ask my questions and listen to your answers."

The wizened soothsayer huffed again and studied the young witch with an intensely appraising gaze. He glanced at Nancy, his upper lip curling into a grimace of irritation. "I don't like her."

Nancy spread her arms a little and shrugged.

"She can stay." With a grunt, Astro abandoned the manufactured search through his desk drawer and thumped his cane across the floor. He moved slowly toward Laura standing behind the closest armchair, but she waited patiently with a small, self-assured smile. When the soothsayer reached her, he stopped only a few inches from Nancy Milton's oldest daughter and sniffed at the space between them. "Your sisters asked too many questions. Am I gonna get the same flailing attempt from you?"

Laura tilted her head and didn't flinch. The soothsayer stood so close, she could smell the old age on him. "I already know exactly what kind of information I'm looking for, so probably not."

"Heh." Astro smacked his wrinkled lips again and peered up at her. "You're as sure of yourself as *she* was."

He nodded toward Nancy, then shuffled across the study, turned around with achingly exaggerated slowness, and lowered himself into the other armchair graced with a convenient side table. The creaking that filled his study could have come from the chair itself or the soothsayer's joints or both.

Nancy smirked at her daughter. "This one would have you think that's a bad thing. But as I remember it, being so sure of myself landed me with an apprenticeship that didn't exist before I came along. And it was obviously enough to make two hours a week of my time worth a few hairs on his precious head."

"Milton, you now hold the record as the only person I know to use that phrase literally."

Laura couldn't decide what phrase he was referring to specifically. *He's deflecting.*

"Speaking of time, Dr. Know It All." Astro pointed a crooked finger at the young witch, one of his dark, beady eyes twitching as he studied her. "The hour your dear mommy promised me doesn't start until you're gone. Got it?"

When Laura glanced at her mom, Nancy offered a little shrug and quickly sat in the other armchair across from her former mentor. "Take as much time as you need."

Laura nodded. Without an extra chair in the study offered to any more than one guest at a time, the oldest Hadstrom sister moved toward the desk and grabbed the rolling office chair behind it that, oddly enough, smelled like freshly baked bread. She quickly wheeled it back toward the armchairs, stopped beside her mom, and sat.

Astro scoffed. "Yeah. Make yourself at home, why don't ya?"

The young witch folded her hands, placed them on her lap, and leaned forward.

It took the soothsayer under fifteen seconds to pull away from Laura's gaze and glance around the room in confusion. He even turned back to look over his shoulder before staring at Nancy and pointing at her daughter. "What's she doing?"

"Waiting until you're ready to tell me what I want to know."

"Ha!" Astro shook a crooked finger at her and cackled. "Like a rabbit in a snare, eh? Like a fingerbone in a big, bubbling, blistering bowl of stew. Fine then, Dr. Hadstrom. Ask your questions."

"Thank you."

In the armchair beside her, Nancy sat back, folded her arms, and prepared herself for what she knew would be the most entertaining discussion she would ever witness with her former mentor. And for once, she wouldn't have to say a word.

CHAPTER FIFTEEN

"The Gorafrex knew enough about the Tenebantur to build it successfully," Laura began. "Leonidas told me he didn't know how the thing found the recipe, but he swore he hadn't kept it written down anywhere."

"Of course, he didn't. The man's not a complete idiot." Astro propped both hands on the head of his cane and sat up straight in his armchair. "A little soft on his customers, unless he's somehow figured out how to grow a spine. But not an idiot."

"I know. Either way, the Gorafrex knew exactly what ingredients it needed for the spell, and it tore Brightwing Emporium apart to create its Tenebantur potion. It makes me think that creature has a lot more knowledge than any of us gave it credit for. I have a theory, but I want to ask you anyway, to be sure."

"You can cut it out with the grand openings and all the build-up, witch." Astro leaned even farther forward, both hands still on his cane, and blinked. "Ask already."

"If everyone who knew about the Tenebantur is more or less sworn to secrecy about a banned potion *you* created two hundred years ago, how did the Gorafrex know all the ingredients and exactly how to set it all up?" Laura frowned. "It's a pretty complicated process."

"What would *you* know of the process?" Astro grumbled.

"Since I watched the Gorafrex make the entire potion and set the Tenebantur—as its prisoner and with my hands tied behind my back—I'd say I probably know enough."

Astro sniffed and fell into another round of hacking coughs. It stopped as suddenly as it had started, then he smacked his mouth over and over and closed his eyes. "That's probably my fault."

"What?" Nancy perked up in her chair and stared at the soothsayer.

"Oh, not intentionally. Don't get your wand all twisted." Astro waved her away and settled in his chair, drawing a deep breath. "It comes with the territory of seeing and unseeing. There are potions, and then there are intentions. And everything in between is one giant, stinky pot of soup. Throw everything together in there and see what you can fish out."

Laura shook her head. "I'm not following all the soup analogies."

"But that little troublemaker sister of yours would, wouldn't she?" Astro threw his head back for another cackle, thumping his cane a few times. "Oh…whoo. She wanted to rip my head right off my shoulders. Threatened to take my cane instead."

"Well, Emily's not here." Laura waited for the old man's

next fit of laughter to die before she decided to repeat herself. "How did the Gorafrex know about the Tenebantur? In a plain explanation without a bunch of metaphors, please."

The soothsayer snorted. "Not one to think very far outside the magical box, are you?"

"Astro," Nancy warned.

"Blah, blah, blah. Let me get there in my time." He jerked a finger toward each of the Hadstrom witches in his study. "Neither of you are blind. I'm an old man."

Laura and her mom humored him enough to sit quietly and wait for the soothsayer to gather his thoughts. He sat there for so long with his eyes closed, his breathing slow and steady, that Laura started to think he'd fallen asleep. She glanced at her mom, then leaned forward to check.

The man's cane thumping on the floor startled her back into the office chair, which rolled back a little across the dusty wood floor. "Seeing isn't a science, you know. Now potions, yes. A basic understanding of alchemy should be taught in every school across the country if you ask me."

"I think it's called chemistry," Laura muttered.

"Oh, is it? If you'd learned anything useful before you went and got all fancy-schmancy Ph.D. on everybody, you wouldn't need me to tell you anything." Astro snorted. "Don't talk until I'm finished. Now, where was I?"

Laura pressed her lips together and drew a deep breath. *Stay calm, and you'll get more than you need out of this guy.*

Nancy closed her eyes with an irritated sigh. "Alchemy as science."

"Yes! That. Anyone can whip up a potion, although it takes a certain level of skill and understanding, like anything else that can and should be mastered. Scrying, on the other hand, is a specialty. You're born with it or you aren't, and there are no takesies-backsies."

Laura blinked and fought not to shout at the old man to get to the point. *I totally get why Emily threatened to take his cane.*

"I've stuck my head into the soup of time and space and intention so many times, it's impossible that I didn't leave behind some of my flavor in the process." Astro waved a dismissive hand toward Laura and nodded. "And before you tell me to cut it out with the soup analogies, this one isn't a figure of speech. I'm talking about the literal soup here."

The soothsayer's cane lifted from the ground, and Astro jerked it toward the far end of the study.

Laura quickly searched the bookcase, then her gaze fell onto the marble basin in front of it and the thick, pea-green liquid simmering in it without any actual heat beneath it—real fire, magical fire, or otherwise. "That's your scrying pool."

"Look at that, Milton!" Astro kicked his brown loafers against the floor in glee. "Maybe you added something to the collective intelligence after all. I bet this one gets all her brains from her dad."

Laura and Nancy glanced at each other and choked on restrained laughter at the same time.

"Maybe it's funny to you now." Astro nodded toward Nancy. "I caught your mother trying to *drink* the damn stuff in that pool."

Nancy closed her eyes and let out another despondent sigh.

"I didn't come here to talk about my mom, though." Laura gestured toward the marble basin in front of the bookshelf. "So, you're saying your knowledge of the Tenebantur somehow...what? Seeped out of you and entered the scrying pool?"

"Soup of space and time and intention. Isn't that what I said?" Astro scratched the side of his face. "It happens. There are very few magicals still around who would have anything close to the type of skill the Tenebantur requires. And there are even fewer soothsayers who'd know what they pulled out of that swamp of scrying knowledge, even if they managed it."

"The Gorafrex isn't either one of those."

"No." The soothsayer turned in his chair to eye his scrying pool as well and let out a long sigh. It ended with another round of coughing, but it wasn't nearly as violent as the last. "The *Gorafrex* isn't bound by physical laws, is it? Not of this ship. Not of Arenya V before the ship set out to fail miserably on its first and only voyage. Not even of wherever else those nasty creatures came from before they found themselves with a taste for your type of magic, eh? But as far as I can see..." Astro tittered and shook his head. "That's funny. As far as I can see, that creature had thousands of years to itself, locked away in that prison. That's thousands of years physically contained in a space it was never and will never be equipped to withstand. And thousands of years to reach out into the ether and explore that way."

Laura blinked and tapped a few fingers against her lips. "You mean it found the Tenebantur, the one *you* created, because it has access to your scrying soup?"

"Access to time and space and—"

"Intention. Yeah, I get it." Laura stared so intently at the soothsayer's marble basin that Astro clearly understood what she wanted.

"Well, go on, then, Dr. McCurious." The soothsayer waved toward the basin. "Go see whatever you're trying to see. Just don't try to drink it."

He let out another cackle and shook his head vigorously as Laura stood and walked toward the scrying pool by the bookshelf. "So, the Gorafrex can access anything that a soothsayer can."

"Not necessarily. It was probably more of a happy mistake for that blood-magic-thirsty creep. Stumbled upon the Tenebantur somewhere inside whatever memories of mine leaked out into the spread of existence. For most people, that's all scrying really is."

Laura frowned down at the slowly bubbling froth inside the basin. Thin tendrils of white smoke lifted from the noxious-looking surface. *Something tells me that's not steam.*

She looked back at Astro and tried her hand at as much flattery as she could stomach. "For most people. But not for you."

"Ah. Aha! Oh…you…" Astro slapped his knee and thumped the cane back down on the floor before pushing himself to his feet again. "I take it back. Maybe I like you a little. Don't let it go to your head, Dr. Butter Him Up with Compliments. You want to see what the Gorafrex knows, do ya?"

"No." Laura rolled her shoulders back and watched the

soothsayer make his slow, laborious way toward her. "I want to see what the Gorafrex *doesn't* know."

"You want—I could die now and say I've finally met someone worthy of a tiny *spec* of admiration." Astro pinched his thumb and forefinger together in front of one squinting eye, then chortled and finished the long trek toward the scrying pool. "That might be the only thing worth wanting to know. Well done."

"Can you show me?"

"Absolutely not."

Laura blinked at him. "Fine. What do you want in exchange?"

"Hold on." Nancy stood quickly from the armchair and headed toward them. "Laura, this isn't the right time to—"

"Can it, Milton." Astro rolled his eyes. "I'm not making a deal with this one."

"Why not?" Laura stuck her hands on her hips. "You told me you admired me."

"And you asked if I *could* show you, not if I *would*. Maybe I spoke too soon." He shook a finger at her, then fell into another round of coughing.

Nancy stopped halfway across the study and folded her arms. When Laura met her mom's gaze, she received the same stern look that tended to precede a long lecture whenever any of the Hadstrom girls had completely messed up. *But, we're not kids anymore. She won't say anything. Not now, anyway.*

Astro finally caught his breath again and struck the side of the marble pool with his cane. "I wouldn't show you even if I could. The Gorafrex has had a lot longer than any of us to sit around with nothing to do but expand its consciousness out into the ether, if not the rest of its…not-body, eh? Showing you what it *doesn't* know would drive you madder than I am."

Laura smirked. "You seem to be holding yourself together pretty well."

"Thank you. I'm a good actor. Now. You won't be writing up a list of what the Gorafrex doesn't know, but I may be able to show you what it doesn't *want* to know. What it's trying to forget or what it's already forgotten after so much time spent going nowhere and looking in every other direction. A thirst for revenge will do that." Astro bobbed his head and knocked the basin with his cane a few more times. "And for blood magic, now that I think about it. Milton."

Nancy raised her eyebrows and waited for her former mentor to finish addressing her.

"I can only assume you remember where the postulous is."

Laura's mom cocked her head. "As long as I can assume that you haven't had a maid in here or done any redecorating in almost thirty years."

"Ha! This is fun, isn't it? Both of us assuming the worst of each other?" The soothsayer pointed his cane at his former student, then stabbed it at the hallway beyond his study. "Go get it."

Nancy stayed long enough to offer Laura a questioning glance.

"I'm fine, Mom."

"Mm-hmm." With one more pointed glance at the soothsayer, Nancy unfolded her arms and turned to hunt through Astro's house for this postulous.

"So. She married that brain-addled Gregory, did she?"

Laura shot the soothsayer a disappointed frown. "That would be more impressive if all three of her daughters didn't have his last name."

Astro snickered. "It would, wouldn't it?"

CHAPTER SIXTEEN

By the time Nancy returned to the study—which couldn't have been more than five minutes later—Laura was convinced the soothsayer had fallen asleep on his feet. Astro had taken up the same position as in his armchair, one hand folded over the other on the cane's head, his eyes closed and his breathing slow and even. The man's head had fallen so low toward his chest, all the extra skin of his neck bunched up under his chin to make him look at least ten pounds heavier. And she could have sworn she'd heard him snore once or twice.

"Snap out of it, old man." Nancy approached her daughter and the almost-asleep soothsayer beside the scrying pool, then held out a small, thin square vial the size of a half-dollar coin. "Here."

Astro didn't move. Laura looked up at her mom and wrinkled her nose. "Is he—"

The soothsayer's wrinkled hand shot out from where he'd propped it and snatched the vial from Nancy's hand. Another slow breath like a snore puttered from between his lips, but he held the square vial out by his side and slowly drew it away from his former student.

"Borderline narcoleptic?" Nancy said flatly. "A lifelong insomniac? So disturbed by polite conversation that he'd rather pretend to be asleep? We'll never know."

Laura fought back a laugh and watched the soothsayer rouse himself from his sleeplike state.

"I hope you haven't spent thirty years trying to figure *that* one out, Milton."

"Trust me, I had much more important things to do with my time. Not sure about you, though."

Astro snorted and finally opened his eyes, made even darker by so many folds of wrinkles around them. "You took that whole mothering thing so seriously, didn't you? *That* is what I don't understand."

When Laura blinked up at her mom, Nancy closed her eyes and shook her head, writing off the whole conversation.

Yeah. It's probably better that way.

"Now, you know exactly what we're missing before we embark on this completely unknown journey through the proverbial soup." Astro extended the square vial toward Laura. When she took it gingerly, he snapped his fingers with a sharp crack and wiggled his fingers over his open palm. "Cough it up."

"I..." Laura jiggled the vial in her hand. "This?"

"Bah. Do I have to do everything myself? Don't answer that. The answer is always yes." The soothsayer moved faster than he should have been able to and snatched Laura's other hand.

She wanted to jerk it away. Astro's fingers were cold,

clammy, and felt more like a soggy piece of bread than flesh and bone. But, she resisted the urge and let him grasp her hand with both of his. His cane toppled over and clattered to the floor. With a barely contained sigh, Nancy bent and picked up the cane, holding it ready for whenever her former mentor demanded to have it back.

The force of Astro's grip would have pulled Laura completely off-balance if she hadn't been trying so hard not to pull her hand away. Without his cane, the old man used her to support his weight as he shuffled around the side of the scrying pool to step right into the Hadstrom witch's personal space. His tongue darted in and out of his mouth, wetting dry and wrinkled lips. Then he grabbed Laura's thumb and yanked it toward his face.

"Woah, hey." Laura steadied herself and watched the soothsayer studying her legacy ring as if he had it under a microscope.

"This is what your father left you." It clearly wasn't a question or a guess. "And one for each of your sisters, eh?"

"Yes."

Astro bent his head and stopped right before he would have mashed his eyeball against her ring. "The original rings from the first Hadstroms of your line. All the way back to the beginning. Yes. Have you ditched the wands, yet?"

"Right before magic stopped working." Laura leaned her head away a little when Astro's jerked up so he could study her face. *Maybe he knows, maybe he doesn't. But I'm not gonna offer up any more information about how magic stopped working unless he asks.*

"Right. Well, anyone who's not a complete moron hasn't

been using their wands in this city for at least a week. I never liked 'em, anyway." Without any warning, the soothsayer jerked Laura's thumb toward his face again and swiftly licked the band of her silver legacy ring—along with most of her thumb.

"Oh..." Laura scowled and automatically wiped her thumb on the side of her cargo shorts once the soothsayer released her hand. "Was that necessary?"

Astro wiggled his fingers and nodded at the square vial in her other hand. With the other, he reached out to grasp the cane Nancy was already handing back to him. Laura started to give the old man the vial until her mom added, "Open it first."

"Really?" It was an automatic reaction, but the young witch did as her mom instructed anyway. The cork was tiny, but she managed to pry it out of the vial before handing the square-shaped glass to Astro.

He quickly took it and lifted the opening on the long neck toward his lips. Laura had to look away when she realized he was spitting into the tiny bottle, and she wished she could turn her hearing off as easily.

"Yes, that's so mature of you." Astro wiped his glistening mouth with the back of a hand and snickered. "You've been running around without magic, trying to fight a creature with nothing to lose, and an old man's spittle is too much for you to handle. No wonder you haven't finished this on your own by now."

Laura handed over the tiny cork, keeping her eyes off the vial as Astro stoppered it one more time and shook it vigorously. The motion made the loose skin under his chin and around his neck wobble violently, and by the time he was finished, he was breathing heavily and on the verge of another coughing attack. But, he held the vial up for all of them to see. The glass had filled with a thick, syrupy silver liquid tinged with a light blue.

"That worked quite nicely. What would you give it, Milton?"

Nancy shrugged. "Seven and a half."

"Seven and a half. Ha! At least you haven't completely wasted the last few decades of your life. Stopped caring about hurting my feelings, have you?"

"Once I realized that's impossible to do, yeah." Nancy Milton and her former teacher locked gazes in a silent stare that made Laura want to back away and duck for cover. Then a tiny smile twitched at the corner of her mom's mouth, and Astro burst out laughing again.

"The next two years are going to be highly entertaining for me, witch. You should know that."

"Wish I could say the same, soothsayer."

"No, you don't." Astro tapped the marble basin with his cane again. "Give it room to breathe. I have no idea what's about to spew out at us next."

"Out of what?" Laura staggered backward when her mom grabbed her wrist and pulled her away from the basin.

The old soothsayer muttered something at the square vial, which he'd pressed almost to his lips but not actually against them. Then he shuffled backward away from his scrying pool as well. "Bottoms up."

His wizened knees cracked when he bent them and tossed the entire vial into the scrying pool. It landed in the thick, bubbling substance with a plop and disappeared.

Astro nodded at the basin, his eyes wide and eager. Nothing happened.

"Takes a while to eat through things," he muttered as if that explained any of what he'd just done. "Now that I think about it, we might be here for—"

A bright blue light burst from the center of the green goop in the pool. It flattened the surface of the substance, erasing the bubbles and the small tendrils of smoke before turning the entire liquid the same bright blue color. It shimmered, pulsed with another wave of light, and let off one massive blue cloud of smoke.

"He turned a scrying pool into a giant potion..." Laura whispered. "What is he—"

"Watch." Nancy gave her oldest daughter's shoulders a reassuring squeeze and gazed at the glowing blue pool. "I've only seen this twice."

The blue smoke billowed from the surface of the scrying pool, and a snaking tendril of it broke apart from the main body. It undulated slowly through the air toward Astro, who gripped his cane again with both hands and broke into a toothless grin. "Here we go, kids. Pay attention!"

As soon as he said it, he drew a deep breath through his nose and drew the extra filament of blue smoke into his lungs. That inhale lasted longer than it should have been able to, but when the soothsayer drew the last of the smoke into his body, the study fell remarkably silent.

Astro let out a sigh that was equally as long, and the same blue glow from the scrying pool illuminated at the back of his throat, reaching out from his open mouth. As he opened his eyes, there was no mistaking that they glowed the same color as he stared at the pool and the shimmering column of smoke rising from his latest spell.

"Watch, listen, and take heed." The soothsayer's voice didn't belong to Astro anymore. It was a chorus of thousands of voices, high and low and inhuman, speaking all at once.

Laura shot her mom a sideways glance and whispered, "Is this supposed to happen?"

"Probably."

CHAPTER SEVENTEEN

"Back to the beginning." Astro's multilayered voice filled the study. "When this sphere thrived on enterprise and hope. The dawning of a new age across the universe."

From the column of smoke in the center of the scrying pool appeared an image only slightly darker than the rest of the light blue glow. Laura squinted and leaned forward to try making it out. "That's the ship."

Her mom nodded.

"And still, not yet separate enough from the longing and the driving force of insatiable hunger." As Astro spoke with his otherworldly voice, the images inside the column of smoke morphed and changed. "What was meant as a sanctuary for one race became, under duplicity and stolen space, a breeding ground for that hunger. The fuel for a being that would never be sated."

Laura tensed when a loud, frantic drumbeat filled the room, but she quickly realized it was much different than the ancient rhythm of the real Gorafrex's luring call. *These drums are coming from the scrying pool. He's talking about the Gorafrex that snuck onto this ship before it set out from Arenya V.*

"What was not part of the original design became a source of fear and hidden knowledge. In this beginning, very few realized what they had accepted into this apparent paradise hurtling across the stars. But the three, bound by duty and fortitude strengthened through empathy, sought the wisdom of this sphere's creators."

The smoke flashed with the only-too-recognizable images of different races on the ship—the shorter, stockier Huldus; their taller, lankier Kashgar cousins; the giant, towering figures of the Velikan Engineers. Then the images faded away to be replaced by three regular-looking people. They could have been anyone, any race, but the long, thin extensions along one of each figure's hands gave them away.

The original Hadstroms. Laura stared at the smoke, trying not to blink so she didn't miss any of the projection's subtle changes.

The multitude of voices continued from Astro's mouth. "The solution was born as all solutions are. Through trust and understanding and a willingness to provide when providing seemed all but impossible. The creators could not conjure from nothingness in the same way they'd come to know before setting out so far from home. So, they turned to what was already created."

The sound of a hammer slamming down on metal rang through the soothsayer's study. Figures of every size and form moved through the blue smoke, working together, mining and crafting, building and casting spells in a quick series of flashing images.

"The solution became the heart of what it was created to resolve. A prison and a sacrifice binding The Three to a past even they could not see. They shoved it away beneath the surface of ignorance and complacency, hoping to restore the paradise they were so sure would remain unthreatened."

Laura's skin prickled when the smoke swirled again to reveal a remarkably detailed vision of the Baron Creek Greenbelt at the heart of Austin. There was the creek itself, the shallow and wide bank, and the huge willow tree growing from a berm in the center of the water. *The prison.*

"But, attempting to erase such a memory living inside the very core of what made The Three who they were was nothing but a naïve and false belief. They used the heart beneath the earth to imprison the being they did not see reflected in their eyes. To push aside their ancestry and the misfortune of such a creature unrecognized, and hence unwelcomed."

A screeching wail rose from the scrying pool, accompanied by those three smoky figures of the original Hadstrom witches and wizards. Bright blue flashes illuminated the tips of three outstretched wands and the centers of three darkened bands. A door slammed shut in an echoing cavern, the wailing faded, and all the images disappeared from within the smoke.

"The Three celebrated a false victory." The voices issuing from Astro's open mouth now sounded tired, even sad. "They did not understand. To lock away their enemy's mindless, unending hunger was to lock away their freedom. Forgotten. Buried. Yet undiscovered despite everything they thought they knew. The heart beneath the earth from which they drew their strength binds the blood to itself. It binds time within the circle, as endless as the prison they did not know contains them still. It binds the past to the future, the healing to the wound, the isolation to the never-ending loop of unity. There can be no safety if there is no threat. No reconciliation without the truth written in blood and flesh and the energy contained. The Three must heal a fourth, and all will become one. It is the—"

Astro stopped short, cleared his throat a few times, then fell into another vicious attack of hacking coughs. He rocked back and forth on his feet, steadying himself with his cane. In a few seconds, he was wheezing to catch his breath between choking on his breath.

"Should we help him?" Lily asked her mom.

"He's fine." Nancy stepped aside and eyed her former mentor with tense curiosity. "But it wouldn't be a bad idea to grab that office chair, in case."

"Yeah." Laura moved quickly as Astro kept hacking up a lung. Her mom stopped her from wheeling right up to the old soothsayer and held up a finger for Laura to wait.

The man threw his head back and took a long, halting breath like he was about to sneeze. Then, with a final cough, he rocked his head forward again. The glowing blue light vanished from his eyes right before a ball of the same-colored light flew from his mouth toward the scrying pool. It hit the column of pulsing blue smoke shimmering over the basin. Then the smoke sucked back down into whatever substance the man kept in that marble basin. There was a loud hiss, a tiny pop, then nothing. The scrying pool was that same pea-green sludge again, which picked right up where it had left off and bubbled slightly as if it had still been simmering all this time.

"There. Ha. You see?" Astro slammed his cane into the ground again and nodded once. "What a load of crap, right? Of *course,* the Gorafrex wouldn't want to remember—"

The soothsayer faltered on his frail, thin legs.

Nancy tapped the office chair and nodded toward him. "Go."

Laura didn't hesitate before quickly rolling the chair across the floor toward the old man. Astro reached out with one hand, finally managed to grasp the armrest of the desk chair, and dropped into it like he couldn't have held himself up any longer. He bounced a little on the cushion and groaned.

Stepping back away from the soothsayer and the scrying pool, Laura waited for the rest. No one said a word. "Is that it?"

"Hmm." Astro cocked his head and thoughtfully smacked his lips again, gazing around his study. Laura couldn't begin to imagine what he was tasting after his unconventional storytelling. "Yep. That's it. I can count on one hand the number of times I stop after finishing a sentence. And this wasn't one of them. Annoying, isn't it?"

Laura stared at the scrying pool and took a hesitant step toward it. "But, what if the end of that sentence is important?"

"It never is." The soothsayer waved off her question and cleared his throat again. "Only some self-evident warning that can be picked out of all that wordiness, anyway. You don't need it."

"How can you know that?"

"Because you have everything else!" He slammed his cane against the floor again and glared at her. Then he broke into a fit of tittering that brought the only color Laura had seen so far rising to his sallow, wrinkled cheeks. "Look, witch. That's as much as you're gonna get with the question you asked. What doesn't the Gorafrex know or want to know? The answer's in all that mumbo jumbo. Now it's your job to pick it apart and figure out what *you* can do about it. Anything else?"

Laura drew a deep breath and forced her rising temper back down where it belonged. "I don't suppose you'd be willing to translate the mumbo jumbo for me."

"Suppose away. You'd be right." Astro slapped a knee and grinned that toothless grin. "I *do* know a prophetic translator who'll charge you an arm and a leg to sort through all that nonsense for you. If he's even still alive. You interested?"

"No, thanks."

The frustrated witch's mother smothered another small chuckle.

Laura ignored her mom and added, "One last question, and then I'll get out of here so you two can start your hour of…whatever."

"Then try to make it a good one, at least, eh?" Astro squealed in amusement as his flat-falling joke.

"Can you tell me anything about how to lock up the

Gorafrex again? When magic starts working again and our rings can actually do what they were meant to do, we need to know how to put it back in that prison, which was obviously a big part of that whole weird visual story." Laura pointed absently at the scrying pool.

"Nope."

"Nope?"

"I can't tell you how to imprison that stealthy creature with no body. Better?" Astro leaned forward against his cane and struggled to keep the office chair from rolling backward across the floor. "Whatever knowledge that *weird visual story* holds is for you and your ring-wearing siblings. That's it. Once you figure out what it is, my guess is you won't have any more questions. So, good luck. Now get out of my house."

"Is he serious?" Laura turned to her mom with wide eyes.

"Yep."

"But none of that made any sense."

"I know." Nancy shot the old soothsayer a warning glance before grabbing her oldest daughter's shoulders and guiding Laura out of the study and into the entryway. "And he also meant every word."

"The insulting parts, too?"

They reached the front door, and Nancy lowered her voice. "Yes, even those. But his bark's harmless compared to everything else. If Astro said you'll find your answers in that riddle of a story he scried for you, then that's where your answers are. You simply have to sort through all the babble."

"Mom. It was all babble."

Nancy drew a deep breath, let it out, and smiled. "If I didn't know how gifted the old man really is, I'd probably agree with you. There's probably something else you'll have to find. Either to turn that whole load of nonsense into something you and your sisters can use or to point you in the right direction toward the next piece of the puzzle. Which you're very good at, Laura, although we both know I don't have to remind you of that. You'll figure it out."

Laura blinked quickly, nodded, then pulled open Astro the soothsayer's front door. Then she turned back toward her mom to wrap Nancy in a tight, quick hug. "Thanks, Mom. For bringing me here and letting me take up more of your Friday night than you probably wanted to spend with this goon."

Nancy chuckled. "An hour goes by quickly for me, sweetheart. I've mastered the art of deflection and keeping a thick skin for just about everything. I'm glad that your sisters got you out of there. Now it's time for you to help them and figure out how to put this whole thing back together the right way."

"I promise I will."

"Oh, I know." Nancy winked and waited for her daughter to step over the threshold and onto Astro's front stoop.

The minute Laura was out of the house, the front door shut behind her. She headed down the walkway toward the sidewalk, lost in her jumbled thinking as she tried to piece together any of what those hundreds of otherworldly voices had recounted through the soothsayer's mouth.

Then she realized she was standing in front of her mom's new Camry and puffed out a sigh.

"Great. I should've driven my car." She pulled her phone out of her purse and scrolled through her recent calls list to find Nickie's number. "It's better than an Uber."

CHAPTER EIGHTEEN

"I should start charging for carpools, huh?" Nickie grinned as she pulled away from Bowman Avenue and headed toward downtown.

In the passenger seat, Laura rolled her eyes. "Oh, yeah? You'd make your sister pay you for a ride?"

"Totally. For this trip, let's call it an even twenty-nine dollars and seventy-three cents."

A sharp laugh of surprise burst from Laura's mouth. "Oh, yeah. Nice and even. Where'd you come up with *that* number?"

"It's a third of the grocery bill." Nickie reached into the center console and whipped out a long receipt from Central Market. She slapped it down into Laura's lap and nodded. "If that list doesn't make Emily a happy cook in her kitchen, I don't know what will."

"Very nice." Laura scrolled through the itemized list. "Chevre? What the heck is chevre?"

Nickie shrugged. "Some kinda cheese, maybe? But it

was in this display that said, 'For the Gourmet Chef in Everyone,' so I figured it couldn't hurt."

"Or it's something she'd be totally insulted to have around."

They both laughed, and Nickie rolled the car to a stop at the next red light. "Hey, if that's the case, we'll just play it off as a joke. So."

"So." Laura set the receipt back in the center console and dropped her head back against the headrest.

"How was your little chat with the crazy old soothsayer?"

"You mean Mom's super-talented potions teacher?"

Nickie chuckled. "Is that what she called him?"

"No. She didn't have to. Apparently, he's one of the best soothsayers around, too. But I'm not really convinced."

"What did he say?"

Laura scrunched her eyes shut and tried to drum up the memory of exactly what all those voices had told her. "Some history about the original Hadstroms making the Gorafrex prison and the rings and everything. Something about being bound to blood and not realizing that they were locking up themselves in that prison, too."

"That doesn't make sense."

"I know." The oldest Hadstrom sister looked out her window at all the other cars and the houses flashing past them. "I'll probably be able to pick out something important we can use. I need a little more time to think about it."

"Or maybe you need to get out, unwind, and enjoy a fun night out on a Friday." Nickie glanced quickly at her sister and wiggled her head. "You know what they say. It's always important to treat yourself after being kidnapped by a witch-killer and narrowly escaping with your life."

Laura chuckled. "Huh. I haven't heard that one before."

"It's trending. Seriously, though, I know a pretty talented blues-rock guitarist who got a last-minute gig at the Mean-Eyed Cat. She's pretty new around here, but I've heard good things."

The oldest Hadstrom sister shot Nickie a sideways glance and coy smile. "Chuck set it up for you, huh?"

Nickie laughed. "Yep. He called me before you did. I'm on at eight-thirty. Wanna come?"

Laura wrinkled her nose and let out an indecisive hum.

"Oh, come on." Nickie drummed her fingers on the steering wheel. "I know the last few times you've tried to go out and have a good time were interrupted by…emergencies." Laura snorted. "But, we've taken care of the Gorafrex problem for right now. Magic is gonna start coming back together any day now. There's literally nothing super urgent that can interrupt a fun night at our favorite bar. Especially when your favorite sister's playing live. Come hang out and have a few drinks. Nachos…"

"Okay, fine." Laura leaned away from her sister as Nickie did a flailing happy dance in the driver's seat. "And please focus on driving."

"I'm so focused." Nickie bobbed and wove to a tune only she could hear, grinning. "You don't even know. Hey, you should bring Nathan too."

"He'd probably really like that."

"Who wouldn't?"

"Are you heading over there right now?"

Nickie nodded. "Yep. Gonna meet Chuck there for a

snack or something. Say hi to the owners. Test out their equipment."

"Okay. Can you drop me off at home, first? I definitely won't be able to relax and enjoy myself if I'm still covered in ripped-through-the-earth-by-glowing-trees."

"Laura, it's very you."

"Ha, ha. It's on the way. Please?"

Nickie jabbed her sister's arm with her elbow and nodded. "You got it. Just make sure you're there by nine so you guys can get a good seat."

"Yep." Laura settled back in the passenger seat and gazed out the window. *A night out with good music and food and Nathan sounds great. Good way for Nickie to unwind, too.*

"Hey, wait." She turned back toward her sister. "Are you playing an acoustic show?"

"Nope."

"But your Strat got all smashed up."

"I know." Nickie grinned and stared at her sister a little too long for Laura's comfort before returning her attention to the road. "I got a loaner for tonight."

"A loaner?"

"Yep. Chuck convinced Straight Music on Ben White to let me borrow their *legend display*."

Laura's smile was all confusion. "I don't know what any of that means."

"The music store, Laura. I guess they think it'll bring in more business for them if they advertise Austin's new Queen of Blues playing a surprise gig at the Mean-Eyed Cat with the actual guitar Calvin Russell played when he came back to the US."

"What? Really?"

"Yep. I don't know how he manages to get everyone on board with stuff like this, but he did it."

Laura smoothed the hair away from her face and reached into her purse for her phone. "Go, Chuck."

"Right?"

"Did you tell Emily about it, yet?"

"Nope. I think she's on 'til eight. Maybe eight-thirty, right?"

Laura pulled up her youngest sister's number to text Emily the details. "Yeah, but she's not gonna want to miss this one. And knowing her, after closing the kitchen tonight, she's gonna want a drink, too."

"Or five."

They both chuckled at that, and Laura sent Emily the text inviting her to join them at the Mean-Eyed Cat once she was off work. Then she pulled up a text to Nathan. "Maybe this *is* exactly what we need, right?"

"Definitely."

"Relax a little and enjoy ourselves after everything that's happened."

Nickie grinned. "Now you're talkin'."

"One night where nothing Gorafrex-related can interrupt us halfway through."

"Woo!"

"Yeah. It'll be fun."

Laura's smile grew even bigger two minutes later when Nathan texted her back.

'Drinks are on me.'

CHAPTER NINETEEN

The Mean-Eyed Cat on W 5th Street was just as busy as could be expected for a Friday night in the middle of May. It was even more packed tonight. Even at 8:30 p.m., when Laura stepped through the doors, she had to push her way through a quickly growing crowd to get to the bar. Apparently, word had gotten out that Nickie Hadstrom was playing a last-minute show just for fun.

"Laura!" Nathan's long arm rose high above all the other heads at the far end of the bar.

She made her way toward him, squeezing through small gaps between people and casting a quick glance at the stage on the other side of the restaurant—a small space beneath the Stag beer sign and the giant TV where the amp and mic were already waiting for Austin's new Queen of Blues. Finally, she reached the end of the bar, and Nathan slid off the stool.

"I really don't mind standing—"

He stopped her with another one of those kisses that made her forget everything she was about to say. The physics professor laughed when he pulled away. "Would you be too upset if I told you I got up for that and wasn't really thinking about where we're gonna sit?"

Laura bit her lip and blinked the kiss-induced mind fog out of her system. "Hard to be upset after a kiss like that."

"That's what I was goin' for." Nathan grinned and gestured toward the only empty seat at the bar now. "And I'm definitely not gonna make you stand. I've been sitting here for twenty minutes, anyway."

"Oh, yeah?" Laura climbed up onto the stool and glanced at shelves of liquor against the back of the bar. Nathan leaned against the old, dinged wood in front of them. "I had no idea you'd be *that* excited."

"I had nothing else going on today. I was about to call you and ask if you wanted to do something tonight. Wasn't sure if you were feeling up to it after…yesterday, so I was really glad you texted me."

"Me, too." She set her forearms on the bar and nodded when the bartender held up a finger to wait a minute. "You know that a little kidnap-and-rescue isn't nearly enough to shut me up in my house for more than a good night's sleep, right?"

Nathan laughed. "I do *now*. And I'm not even a little surprised. You could use a few drinks and some good live music, though. I'm pretty sure that soothes pretty much every issue."

"Almost." *Doesn't get the Gorafrex out of the Clubhouse or put magic back together right-side-up. That would be awesome.*

When the bartender finally reached them, he shot Laura a friendly, energetic smile and nodded. "What can I getcha?"

"A Drink Named Sue, please."

Nathan glanced at her in surprise. "Nice. Yeah, two of those. And you can stick them both on my card and keep that open."

The bartender took Nathan's debit card, then paused and squinted a little at the oldest Hadstrom sister. "You Nickie's sister?"

Laura didn't know why she thought that was so funny, but she laughed anyway. "Yep."

"Cool." The bartender slid Nathan's card back toward him and nodded. "You guys are covered. Be right back."

"We're covered?" Nathan looked genuinely disappointed as he slid his card back into his wallet and his back pocket. "When am I gonna get a chance to buy you a drink on my own?"

"Eventually. Someday. In a place where nobody knows who Nickie Hadstrom is and doesn't make a comment about how much we look alike."

The physics professor bent low over the bar to bring his face a few inches from hers. "We're gonna have to leave Austin for that, aren't we?"

"Or farther, yeah."

Twenty minutes later, the bar was almost too full to make any kind of movement a possibility. Somehow, Emily still made her way toward the end of the bar and clapped her hands down on Laura and Nathan's shoulders at the same time.

The oldest Hadstrom sister jumped in surprise and barely managed to keep the last third of her vodka cocktail in the glass where it belonged. Nathan laughed and turned around. "Hey, Em!"

"Nice turnout tonight, huh?" Emily wiped the sweat off her forehead with the back of her hand and fanned her face. "Whew. I'd say they should've moved this party outside, but it's actually cooler in here even with all the sardined Nickie fans."

"How many people did you have to push over to get to us?"

The youngest Hadstrom sister grinned up at Nathan and shrugged. "At least five. I see you started without me. Awesome."

"Only one, Em." Laura offered her glass. "Wanna try?"

"What is it?"

"Cucumber vodka and something."

"No, thanks."

Nathan made a jokingly suspicious face and squinted at her. "Lemme guess. You're goin' for a…margarita."

"Ha. No. Funny, though. You should let Laura tell you all about the last time we went to see Nickie play and how much fun *she* had with margaritas."

Laura took another large gulp of her drink.

"Okay." Nathan studied Laura's rising blush and laughed. "I'll remember to ask."

"I don't know what you're talking about."

"Come on, Laura. We brought John with us, remember? That night out at Gruene Hall when—"

"You're here!" Chuck skirted the bar with his arms spread wide and a huge, goofy smile plastered all over his face. When he reached them, he stopped to briefly eye Emily up and down. "New look, Em?"

"What, you haven't heard? Sweaty under the armpits and splattered with sauce is totally in right now." Chuck cocked his head and shot her a disbelieving smile. "I just got off work, Chuck. And I didn't wanna risk missing Nickie's opening."

"Yeah, that makes a lot more sense." With a laugh, he raised his hand and nodded at the bartender. "Harry. Hey, Harry!"

"Yeah."

"Sister number three right here. Make sure she's taken care of too, all right?"

"No problem. Be right there." Harry the bartender took a drink order from someone who'd been waiting a lot longer than Emily, and Chuck clapped his hands, looking ridiculously proud of himself.

"Hey, thanks, Chuck." Emily reached her fist toward him, and he bumped it with his own.

"Yeah, well, I might not be the best *apprentice*...yet." Chuck grinned and paused until the people trying to weave through the crowd quit pushing up against his back. "But I'm really good at making sure everybody has a good time. Especially when Nickie's up there doing her thing."

Nathan pointed at him. "I'm gonna remember this, man."

"What?"

"That's right. One of these days when we all go out again, drinks are on me."

"Oh..." Chuck laughed and bobbed his head over and over, drunk already off nothing but his excitement. "Good luck with that."

"You won't even see it coming."

"You do what you gotta do, man." Chuck leaned forward toward the Hadstrom sisters and the professor and glanced from one of them to the next with a conspiratorial smirk. "This is gonna be awesome, guys. Just wait. And I get to watch all this with a brand-new pair of eyes, you know?"

"Uh…" Emily pursed her lips and tried not to burst out laughing over the guy's contagious enthusiasm. "How's that?"

"This is the first show Nickie's played since…I mean, since I found out about everything. You know, the three of you and the whole G-O-R—"

"Oh, *right.*" Emily winked at him. "Gotcha."

"I get why you guys like to keep all that a secret, right? It's crazy. Now *I* know what makes Nickie's playing so *magical…*"

Laura pointed at him and grinned. "Punny."

"And nobody else in the whole bar knows about it. They have no idea she's a…what all three of you are. But I do, and I still get to watch her knock the socks off everybody here. It's so great!"

Emily patted Chuck on the shoulder and finally had to let herself laugh about it. "Good for you, Chuck-o. I'm glad you're so excited."

"Thanks, Em. Okay. Drinks are on me. Order whatever you want if you're hungry, too. Kitchen's open 'til nine. Nickie's coming on any minute, so I'll see you guys after." He grinned at them, slapped the side of Nathan's arm, and disappeared into the crowd.

The Hadstrom sisters looked at each other with wide eyes, and Emily threw her head back for an unrestrained laugh that hardly made a sound in the crowded, noisy bar.

Nathan ran a hand through his dark hair and raised what was left of his drink. "Is he on something right now?"

That only made Emily laugh even harder.

"Nope." Laura looked out over the crowd but couldn't find any sign of Chuck bobbing and weaving through tightly packed patrons. So, she lifted her glass toward Nathan in a silent toast. "He's like this every time Nickie plays."

"Wow." The professor clinked his glass against hers for the second time since they'd gotten their drinks and knocked back the rest of it. "There's a guy who loves what he does."

"Ha." Emily pointed at him. "True on more than one level."

"Emily…" Laura tried to chastise her sister but couldn't quite put her heart into it.

Emily's laughter finally died down enough for her to lean toward her sister and ask, "Hey, you think we should tell him about who showed up to watch her play tonight?"

"Definitely not until after the show."

Nathan took in a sweeping glance of the gathered crowd and chuckled. "You mean because it's mostly witches, wizards, and fairies in here right now?"

"I passed a couple dwarves on the way in," Emily added.

"And Chuck has no idea that most people in here already know Nickie's a witch." Laura raised her glass to her lips and shook her head in amusement. "Most of them probably think *he* still doesn't know."

"Then I have to agree with you, there," Nathan said, raising his eyebrows and surveying the crowd of magicals with no ability to use magic whatsoever—at least for now. "Maybe don't tell him 'til tomorrow or something."

"Yep." Emily leaned toward the bar when she saw Harry the bartender making his way in their direction. "The guy deserves to be excited about something for a little longer than a few hours."

CHAPTER TWENTY

The crowd went nuts inside the Mean-Eyed Cat when Nickie Hadstrom took the stage. She came out with the Calvin Russell guitar strapped around her neck and her favorite lime-green pick in hand. Chuck had been buying them in bulk for at least a year.

"Hey, look at this," she said, laughing into the microphone. "Great turnout, huh?"

The bar erupted again in applause and whistles and cheering.

"I can't tell if you guys crammed yourselves in here tonight to see me play or to see this baby *get* played." She gave the guitar's body a few loving pats, and a round of laughter swept through the crowded bar. "I don't really care either way. I still get to do my thing, right?"

"Yeah, Nickie!" some dude screamed over the cheering.

She chuckled again and nodded in the direction of the voice. "And so does this guy, I guess. Here we go."

Only the first loud, blaring chord she struck was clearly heard before the cheering and whistling started up all over again. But it quickly died down enough for everyone in the bar to follow Nickie Hadstrom's lead and get into the groove of her music. That only lasted until she started singing, and another round of excited cheering washed over the crowd.

"They're really letting it all out tonight." Emily leaned toward Laura and sipped from the straw in her Old Fashioned.

"A whole bunch of magicals without any magic for the last week coming to watch their favorite Queen of Blues witch?" Laura laughed. "Looks like everybody else could use a night without thinking about everything that's wrong with Austin right now."

"Sure does."

Next to the sisters, Nathan bobbed his head to the rhythm of Nickie's first upbeat song. "She's great."

"What clued you in, Nate?"

He made a face at Emily, then dipped his head toward her. "John not coming tonight?"

"He's probably still at work."

Laura frowned at her sister and tried to find the perfect volume between raising her voice and shouting like everyone else. "Did you even invite him?"

Emily stared straight ahead toward the stage and shook her head. "John's definitely on my list of things to forget about tonight, okay?"

"Yeah, no problem." Laura sipped her drink again and shared a curious glance with Nathan.

"And before you start worrying about me and what I'm gonna do about him, we already made plans to go out tomorrow night. So, I'm taking care of it."

"Good to hear."

Nathan bent down to press his lips against Laura's ear so he wouldn't have to keep yelling. "Didn't one of you guys say something about John being a huge Nickie fan?"

Laura nodded with wide eyes. *At least Emily had a good reason not to invite him if he's still working.*

She almost dropped her drink when Nathan snatched up her free hand and tried to pull her off the barstool. With a surprised laugh, Laura tugged back a little. "What are you doing?"

"Getting you on your feet." Nathan grinned. "What, you don't like dancing?"

"Of course, I *like* dancing—what?"

Emily had slipped the glass out of her sister's hand and set it on the bar. "Dance, Laura. Right now! Don't even think about doing anything else."

The oldest Hadstrom sister playfully rolled her eyes but slid off the chair, laughing when Nathan pulled some ridiculous move made even funnier by his height and long arms. But it didn't take her long to ease into the music and let her one and a half drinks do the rest of the loosening up for her.

Nickie made it through three songs before things got weird. When she struck the last chord of that third track, she felt an odd, prickling tingle of energy that shouldn't have been there while she was playing just to rock out. It wasn't big, and the people closest to her and the stage didn't seem to notice anything at all, so she shrugged it off and kept going.

Nothing's as bad as hearing the Gorafrex's drums and getting a migraine mid-set.

Twenty seconds into her next song, the stage started trembling every time she strummed a different cord. The microphone squealed a little without being moved, but it quit when she knocked it with the side of her hand and didn't miss a beat. When she started singing, things seemed fine, so she closed her eyes and lost herself in the lyrics.

Until the air between the microphone and her mouth got incredibly hot.

Nickie opened her eyes and glanced down at the microphone. The metal grid of the mic head was glowing a dull red, quickly growing brighter and, yes, hotter. *Great. Literally on fire with this song. What's going on?*

Fortunately, she was already at the end of the first verse, so she didn't have to cut the singing out of something too obvious. Instead of diving into the second verse, she stepped back and launched into one of her favorite riff solos out of all her pieces. She glanced up, saw a few people who obviously recognized her song and that she was playing it a little differently tonight, and forced a grin.

Just act like it's supposed to happen this way. Not too hard.

She bent over Calvin Russel's guitar—grimacing a little at the sharp pain in her ribs that still hadn't gone away—and let the strings have it, her fingers flying over the fretboard as fast as they always did. Nothing else seemed to be magically burning up, so she slipped right back into the jam and went for it.

Sweat dripped down her forehead and the sides of her neck. The next few measures of her solo sounded a little too echoey. *Who messed with the reverb?*

It was the last thought she had before she picked up on the startled gasps coming from the front row of people there to watch her. *Yeah, I know. It really does sound amazing—*

Nickie sucked in a sharp breath when the callouses on her fingers finally couldn't stand up against the heat beneath them. She opened her eyes and saw all six guitar strings glowing the same dull red as the mic head. Only, they were getting a lot brighter a lot faster. In a last attempt to save the show—and her fingers—she let go of the strings with a final note and jammed the whammy bar, pulling her pick hand back for effect.

The cheer rising after that was only half its usual force, but at least nobody was screaming. *Keep it together, Nickie. You're rockin' it. Do your thing.*

The strings had instantly cooled off, so she grabbed the guitar again and hit it with another blaring cord. Then somebody did scream.

Two of the strings snapped and almost took her cheek with them when they sprang away from the fretboard. The legendary Austin instrument let out a strangled snarl like an angry cat, then the entire body burst into flames.

"What the—"

Nickie jerked the instrument sideways, ducked out of the strap, and tossed the whole thing onto the stage. A round of startled gasps and shouted surprise filled the Mean-Eyed Cat, then the whole place fell eerily silent. Breathing heavily, Nickie stared at the burning guitar that was on loan from Straight Music. She grabbed the pint glass of water off the stool at the back of the stage and dumped the whole thing onto the flaming instrument.

Thankfully, the fire went out like a normal fire despite having caught on an electric guitar through magic in the first place.

Cautiously eyeing the smoking, hissing remains of the guitar, Nickie slowly stepped up to the mic. Looking out over all the wide eyes and dropping jaws, she smirked. "Jimmy Hendrix never managed to pull *that* off."

Laughter and a few cheers rose from the more dry-humored audience members.

"All right," she added, raising her hand to point at the charred and now soaked guitar on the stage. "Let's see what we can do about getting another guitar up here. I promise to be gentle."

Where's Chuck? And what the heck just happened?

"The show must go on, right—woah!" She leapt back away from the sudden burst of flames licking around the head of the mic, and her flailing hand knocked the stand over in the process. The mic fell to the stage with a loud thump and a squeal, and Nickie couldn't keep pretending this was all just part of the plan.

The flames grew to twice their size around the microphone, and then something bright and silver hurtled through the air toward Nickie. It flashed in the bar's low lighting before landing right beside the fallen microphone. Glass shattered, a puff of white light burst over the microphone, and the flames snuffed out.

"All right, everybody. Time to pay attention!" A wide path opened from the other side of the bar, and two Huldu in different shades of gray overalls stepped through with their hands raised. "We all love a good show with lots of flames and destroyed guitars, but that only happens at the end. Mostly."

The slightly taller gnome mechanic cleared this throat and waved the closest people out of the way with a shooing gesture. "And this show is officially over. We're callin' it."

"No!" someone shouted. "You can't shut her down!"

"We just did, fancypants." The shorter Huldu with a scruff of bright-orange hair pointed in the direction of the voice then hopped up onto the low stage in front of a completely bewildered Nickie Hadstrom. "By now, you've all heard about that massive explosion in the middle of downtown last week. Yes, confirmed, it was a Peabrain kid in his own back yard. Blah, blah, blah." The gnome sounded bored at this point, but he didn't look like he was pulling some kind of prank, either. "We've been tasked with making sure nothing else blows up and rattles the city like that again. I'm pretty sure none of you want to get caught up in a mess you won't be able to clean up with any form of magic whatsoever. We're keeping Austin weird, not trying to blow it up weirder."

"Which is why we're calling off the show." A round of groans and boos filled the Mean-Eyed Cat. The taller Huldu with a perpetual squint clapped his hands and rubbed them vigorously together. "Now, who here has absolutely no idea what we're talking about and would like to forget everything they just heard?"

A few confused humans who'd managed to grab themselves a spot at Nickie Hadstrom's last-minute gig slowly, timidly raised their hands. Emily's jaw dropped, then she scowled at the Huldus. *Oh, sure. They give* these *unawakened Peabrains the choice. But not John.*

"Excellent. Come with me, please." The taller Huldu waved the confused humans after him as he made his way back through the aisle parted in the crowd. Three humans followed, and the Hadstrom sisters were glad to see that Chuck wasn't among them. None of them could find him anywhere.

"Okay, kids." The orange-bearded gnome pointed at Nickie without looking away from the surprised and highly disappointed crowd. "Anyone else in this bar calling themselves a Hadstrom these days?"

Laura raised her hand, and Emily folded her arms. "Em, the Huldus are asking for us."

"Oh, really? Huh. I wasn't aware that we owed those mind-erasing gnomes anything at all."

The Huldu on stage next to Nickie nodded. "All right, then. The three of you need to come with me. Everyone else, go back to pretending like you know what's good for you. Harry!"

"Yeah." The bartender lifted his chin and folded his arms with the exact same unamused expression as Emily.

"Get a round for the house and put it on my tab."

A conceding cheer went up from the packed bodies of magicals. Harry the bartender could barely be heard over the excitement at the prospect of a free drink round. "You haven't paid your tab from last month!"

"I'm good for it, Harry. You know that. Little busy right now." The orange-bearded gnome turned toward Nickie, raised an eyebrow, then pointed down at the guitar lying in charred ruins on the stage. "I always liked Calvin Russell. That one of his old guitars?"

Nickie ran a hand through her hair. "Yeah."

The Huldu whistled. "Bummer."

She huffed out a breath of disbelief. "Yeah..."

The gnome hopped off the stage and waved Nickie after him. Then he snapped his fingers and pointed at Laura, Emily, and Nathan at the end of the bar. "We're goin' out back. Don't make me drag you out there, got it?"

Then he disappeared through the crowd and through the back door onto the Mean-Eyed Cat's outdoor patio.

Nickie made her way around the side of the room, smiling and nodding as a few people expressed their feelings about the situation.

"That was awesome."

"Best fire stunt I've seen in a few decades."

"You're gonna go places, kid."

Finally, she met up with her sisters and Nathan halfway to the back door and shook her head. "Sorry, guys."

Laura grabbed Nickie's wrist and leaned toward her. "What happened?"

"I have no idea."

"I thought magic was supposed to start working again with all the energy cores gone," Emily added.

"It's obviously not instant, Em." Laura pressed her back against the door and held it open for her sisters and Nathan. "And now we have a couple of Huldus calling us by name. So, let's see what they want."

Before the door closed behind them, Chuck came racing out of the Mean-Eyed Cat, eyes wide with concern. "Nickie!"

She turned around and couldn't immediately meet his gaze. "Hey."

"What happened? Are you okay?"

"I'm fine."

"Let me see." Chuck grabbed her hands and turned them over to inspect his girlfriend's fingers. They were a little redder than they should have been. "Okay. I'll get some ice."

"Really, I'm fine, babe." Nickie grabbed his hand instead and pulled him with her after her sisters. "Only a little magical weirdness, right?"

"You know, you can't really write this one off as a funny little accident, Nickie. Not when your guitar caught on fire in the middle of a set."

"I know. And I'm so sorry about the guitar. I know you got Straight Music to loan it, and they're gonna be pissed. I'll pay for it, don't worry—"

"Hey, stop." Chuck gently pulled her back toward him and wrapped his arms around her. "That could've been a lot worse. Not for the guitar, but for you. I'm serious. I'm glad you're okay. And let me worry about Straight Music, okay? That's my job."

Nickie chuckled a little. "Explaining how one of your musicians set a borrowed Calvin Russell guitar on fire for no apparent reason? I didn't know you'd added that to the list of career requirements."

"No, I'm talking about the broader umbrella of taking care of all the other boring details, so all you have to do is focus on playing one hell of a show." Chuck leaned away from her a little and grinned. "Which that totally was, by the way. Even with the unorthodox interruption. You were amazing."

"Yeah, okay. Definitely wasn't my best, but thanks—"

"Hey! Lovefest!"

They both looked up to see the orange-bearded Huldu sitting at one of the picnic tables under the string of outdoor lights. Laura, Emily, and Nathan were already seated with him, and the taller Huldu made his way toward the impromptu magical meeting.

"We don't have all night, okay?"

Chuck leaned toward his girlfriend and whispered, "Who's that?"

"Two Huldus who came to break up my show." Nickie squeezed his hand and led him toward the table. "And before you ask, I have no idea what they want."

CHAPTER TWENTY-ONE

Emily stared at the taller Huldu approaching the table on the Mean-Eyed Cat's back patio. The guy's squinty eyes didn't change above a scowl of distaste, but when he noticed the young witch eyeing him, he jerked his head up at her.

"What's with all the mean-muggin'?" He sat at the end of the bench across the table from her and raised his eyebrows.

"What did you do with those Peabrains over there?" Emily nodded behind him toward the group of three humans who'd volunteered to "forget" all the magical announcements after Nickie's interrupted show. They sat in a line of three extra chairs, all of them blinking in confusion as they tried to remember why they were here and what they'd been doing.

"Oh, them?" The gnome gave her a dismissive wave. "They're fine."

"You know what I think?"

Laura nudged her little sister under the table with her shoe. "Careful, Em."

The youngest Hadstrom witch ignored the warning. "I think you flashed a fancy pink light and erased their memories."

"Oh, yeah? That's a random guess, huh?" The gnome slapped his hands onto the wooden table and leaned toward her. "They *wanted* to forget. They all do. And it's a lot safer that way, especially right now. I *asked*, and they volunteered. So, I don't know why you're making such a big deal out of it."

"Such a big deal?" Emily let out a dry, sarcastic laugh. "Is that standard practice for Huldus? To *ask* before you obliterate huge chunks of a Peabrain's memory?"

The gnome squinted even more, then pointed at Emily and looked at Laura. "What's her problem?"

"You might wanna rein it in, Tiberius." The orange-bearded Huldu eyed Nickie and Chuck as they approached the table. "Just for tonight, okay?"

"Yeah, maybe." Tiberius glared at Emily again. "Ronan's tellin' me to rein it in, so I'll rein it in. But I don't like the way you're accusing me of doing my job. Just so we're clear."

"Well, I don't like the way you do your job." Emily sat back on the bench and folded her arms. "Just so we're clear."

"Okay!" The orange-bearded Ronan clapped his hands. "This is obviously the worst way to start a meeting, so I'm gonna try to redirect this thing. What's he doing here?"

Chuck froze beside Nickie when he realized the Huldu was pointing at and referring to him. "Uh…I'm with them."

"Nope. Sorry. No unawakened Peabrains sitting in on this one. Why don't you step aside with my friend Tiberius, here, and he'll tell you all about what happens—"

"No!" the Hadstrom sisters shouted at once.

Ronan blinked furiously at them, and Tiberius smacked a hand against his forehead before rubbing what little hair remained above it. "Okay, this has gotta be good. Explain."

"He knows," Nickie said, slipping her fingers through Chuck's under the table. "About everything. What we are, what we do…what's happening with magic right now."

"What?" Tiberius leaned forward to peer around his fellow Huldu at Chuck. "He's still asleep."

Chuck snorted. "Trust me, I spent days wondering if this was all a dream."

"I mean your little Peabrain hasn't started shooting magic all through your—"

"Yeah, I know what you meant, thanks." Chuck caught the Huldus gaze and nodded. "If you have some secret information that'll help me *wake up*, I'm all ears. But I'm not going anywhere, and I'm definitely not going with *you* for a private chat."

Tiberius blew a raspberry at Nickie's boyfriend, then glanced at Ronan and shook his head. "Sounds like they have it all figured out, huh?"

"You've had a bad day, buddy." Ronan thumped his fellow Huldu on the back. "Let me do the talking for now. So. As you probably noticed—wait. What's with the Kashgar?"

On the other side of Laura, Nathan raised his eyebrows and kept a remarkably blank expression. "Part Kashgar, actually."

"No kidding. Yeah, you definitely got the build and something around the eyes..."

"And you know what Bernie would say about that," Tiberius muttered.

"But Bernie's not here, is he? And this isn't his assignment *or* his department, so we'll drop it."

"What's this whole thing about?" Laura asked. Both Huldus jerked their heads up to look at her. "We haven't gotten to that part yet, and I'm definitely ready to hear why two Huldus showed up at my sister's show to ask for all three of us by name."

"I like you." Ronan nodded. "Cutting right to the chase. And the Hadstroms are all good with this sleeping Peabrain and the part Kashgar sitting in on this?"

"Obviously," Emily muttered.

Ronan frowned at her. "Right. You'll have to excuse us for asking all the questions we can think of because nothing's really obvious around here right now, is it?"

"Not when you keep stalling."

"Emily..."

"Yeah, okay." Emily lifted her hands in surrender. "I'm done."

"So, here's the rub." Ronan interlaced his fingers, pulled back to crack his knuckles, and set his folded hands on the table. "You've noticed some serious issues in this city with magic in general, which I always hesitate to lump into one giant category. Except for now."

"Forget serious issues," Tiberius cut in. "Magic's broken."

"Okay, friendly reminder, T. Let me talk. So, you've

noticed, the rest of the city's magical community has noticed, clearly. And now we've noticed, too."

"Really?" Nickie bent her head toward Ronan in disbelief. "You're noticing just *now*? Magic hasn't been working for at least a week."

"Oh, we're quite aware of the timeline. Thanks. What I'm talking about is that we've finally managed to connect a few dots and trace some interesting things back to the source. Those of us stationed here have been keeping our eyes wide open since this broken magic is pretty much contained to Austin. For now. But that's our job, right? To keep an eye on things. And your show tonight confirmed what we've suspected for a few days. Which was awesome, by the way. Even with the flaming instrument."

Nickie blinked. "Thanks."

"Don't mention it. Still, a few awesome minutes of killer music doesn't change the fact that all the especially weird incidents around here can be traced back to a few people we never had to pay that much attention to. Okay, so I'll be blunt about it."

"Please do." Laura clasped her hands. "We prefer that."

"Yeah. Uh…okay." Ronan scratched his head, then turned toward Tiberius. The taller Huldu mimed locking his lips and throwing away the key. "Right. Bluntly, simply, without trying to beat around the bush…all the weirdest stuff with magic right now can be traced back in one way or another to the three of you."

Chuck sat up straight and frowned. "You're talking to five of us right now."

"Witches, Peabrain. Hadstrom witches. These three."

Laura, Nickie, and Emily exchanged wide-eyed glances and didn't immediately have anything to say.

"Yeah, so your silence about this is digging this hole even deeper." Ronan drummed his fingers on the table and turned his head back and forth between Nickie sitting beside him and the other two witches sitting across the table. "Time to spill the magic beans, so to speak."

"No." Emily shrugged. "We don't owe these guys anything."

"Hold on, Em." Nickie gestured toward the Huldus beside her. "Maybe they can help."

"They didn't help with John, did they?"

Ronan cocked his head. "Who's John?"

"See? Just proving my point."

"We have to," Laura added. When Emily kept glaring at Tiberius across the table—who obviously wasn't backing down from the provided staring contest—Laura gently set a hand on her sister's shoulder and shook her a little. "Hey."

Emily slowly turned to look at her sister, not amused by any of this.

"I'm not trying to place blame or claim it or anything. Only taking responsibility. None of this would've happened if I'd stayed away from those wards, right? The Huldus already know enough to find us, and it would be completely irresponsible not to tell them what happened. Nickie's right. Maybe they can help."

The youngest Hadstrom sister gritted her teeth, her knee bouncing up and down under the table. Then she shrugged. "Your call, Laura. Whatever you wanna do. I'm not going anywhere, but for the record, I really don't like this idea."

"I know. Neither do I."

"All right." Ronan clapped loud enough to get everyone's attention again. "Now would be the part where you define what *this* actually is, huh?"

Laura nodded at the Huldu. "This is kind of a long story, so fair warning. We might be here a while."

"Uh-huh." Ronan slapped Tiberius' arm with the back of his hand. "Hey, T. Go put in an order of nachos. No, make it two. And a round of beers for everybody. You guys like beer, right?"

A wave of shrugging consent and a few nods passed around the table.

"Good. Go on."

Tiberius frowned at his fellow gnome. "Why do I have to—"

"'Cause it's goin' on my tab, T, okay? And we don't need a repeat of the last time you went all day without eating anything. Do we?"

Grumbling, Tiberius stepped backward over the bench. "Don't start without me."

"Wouldn't dream of it." Ronan folded his hands on the table again and glanced from one Hadstrom sister to another with a reassuring smile. "Would we?"

CHAPTER TWENTY-TWO

"And that's where we are right now." Laura spread her arms after finishing the entire story, starting from the day she took the bronze dagger to the Greenbelt to help her through the wards around the Gorafrex's prison under the willow tree.

The cheese-slathered nacho in Ronan's hand fell back into the paper-lined basket with a splat, and he blinked a few times. "Okay, so let me get this straight. You released a murderous, ethereal body from an iron prison after thousands of years. It killed a witch, took over five Peabrain hosts—"

"That we know of," Nickie interjected.

"Well, five's enough. Magic broke because the Gorafrex charged two energy cores with blood magic—"

"One and a half, actually," Emily muttered.

"I'm rounding up." Ronan briefly pressed a hand to his forehead. "But now you've destroyed an entire Velikan escape vessel beneath the city. Your family has been responsible for keeping that thing locked up and protecting Austin from everything that's basically already happened…and we've never heard of any of you. Does that sound like a well-rounded summary, or am I missing something?"

Chuck stroked his chin and slowly nodded. "Yeah, those are pretty much all the major bullet points."

"And you know all of this *how?*" Ronan leaned far over the table until his orange beard scraped against the cheesy nachos to stare at Chuck. "As an unawakened Peabrain, am I right?"

"I prefer Chuck, honestly."

Emily snorted.

"And yes, I know all this because that Gorafrex thing almost killed me, too. Plus, I think I might have a real knack for potions." Chuck gave a half-hearted shrug and couldn't hide a tiny smile.

"Wow. Now I've heard everything." Ronan rubbed a hand down his face, tugged on his orange beard, and puffed out a sigh. "Okay, so magic's supposed to be coming back online any day now. That's good news."

"That's what we're hoping for." Laura grabbed a loaded nacho from the closest basket and crammed it in her mouth. "At least, that's what Rutilda told me. She did seem to have a few too many loose screws up there, but I'm pretty sure she knew what—"

"Wait a minute. Rutilda *who?*" Tiberius squinted at the oldest Hadstrom sister and slid his bottom jaw sideways until he looked way too much like Popeye.

"Um…" Laura chewed quickly and swallowed. "The Velikan Engineer. I didn't catch a last name."

"The…you've gotta be kidding me." Ronan drained the

last of his beer and let out a huge belch. "I'm gonna be drowning in paperwork on this one for the next few hundred years. You actually spoke to one of the Velikan?"

"Yes. And I'm pretty sure she's the *last* Velikan. Conveniently living right under the—"

"Yeah, we know where she lives. Had to escort her home a little less than a week ago when she decided to spring up out of the ground and go stomping all over Austin."

Emily's head jerked up at that. "You."

"Yes, hello." Ronan blinked at her. "We've all been sitting at this table together for the last hour. You feelin' okay?"

"You were there that night? When Rutilda made it all the way out to Emma Long?" Emily's fists clenched in her lap.

"Didn't make it to the park. I was on cleanup duty, trying to contain the mess she made. Are you *sure* you're not sick or something? Maybe heatstroke? Your face is lookin' *pretty* red."

Emily drew a deep breath and forced herself not to say or do anything she'd regret later. "Do you know who followed her into the park?"

"At least one, yeah. Listen, I thought we were all under the impression that *I* was asking the questions and the rest of you were answering them, not the other way around. When this whole thing's over, you can ask me all about the other Huldu chasing a Velikan who lost her mind a long time ago. Right now, I'd like to focus on the next steps. Mainly how to put magical Humpty Dumpty back together again. Capisce?"

Laura nudged her little sister's foot again and muttered, "Just for now, Em. Until things are back on track."

Emily grabbed the beer she'd hardly touched and took a long gulp.

"Okay, so Ronan missed one major thing." Tiberius drummed his fingers on the table. "Can't really blame him. There's always *something* that falls through the cracks."

Ronan pushed the half-eaten basket of nachos toward his buddy and scowled. "Still hung up, I see. Have some nachos."

Tiberius crunched his fist around a pile of slathered chips and crammed it all into his mouth without looking away from Laura. Cheesy crumbs and a few bits of pulled pork dropped back into the basket. "You spent all this time—"

"Swallow first, man. Come on."

Tiberius chewed quickly, swallowed, and started over. "You spent all this time chasing the Gorafrex around, trying to lock it back up in the prison, and that part's still not finished. So where exactly *is* that thing right now?"

"Well..." Laura glanced at Nickie, who raised an eyebrow. "It's locked up. For now."

"Uh-huh."

"Just not in the prison our ancestors built for it." Nickie circled her finger around the table. "All of our ancestors, actually. So, it's more or less a temporary prison at this point."

Ronan spread his arms and leaned forward. "Which is..."

Laura reached into her back pocket and pulled out her keyring. Nickie and Emily reluctantly did the same, and the three Hadstrom witches all dangled their keys over the table without really wanting to say anything about it.

Ronan scratched his head. "I don't get it. You stuck the thing in three different cars, or what?"

Laura set her keys on the table and separated the silver Clubhouse coin with her thumbprint from the rest of her keys. "We call it the Clubhouse."

"Cute."

She shot Tiberius a quick frown. "Well, it fit, seeing as we made the thing when we were in elementary school."

"And it's holding the Gorafrex." Ronan stuck another nacho in his mouth.

"Yeah. Like I said, for now."

"And the thing can't get out, right?"

Emily snorted. "Didn't know there was an echo out here."

"All right, Grumpypants. Hold on a minute." Ronan lifted his hand toward the youngest Hadstrom witch. "I'm trying to figure out how a treehouse with a lock made by a bunch of kid witches is even remotely powerful enough to keep a creature like a *Gorafrex* from getting back out and ripping the city apart all over again."

Nickie cleared her throat. Laura tapped a finger against her lips and stared at the Clubhouse coin on the table. Emily stared at her sisters, then sighed. "Okay, fine. I'll say it. We didn't build a treehouse. Which is honestly a little lame for three kid witches and kind of insulting. We built a different dimension."

Tiberius turned away from the table just in time to spray beer out of his nose and all over the patio instead of Emily Hadstrom. "You built a *what?*"

"Pretty sure I wasn't mumbling." Emily folded her arms. "A different dimension."

"At least, that's as close to an explanation as we can get," Laura added. "We aren't really sure what it is."

Ronan's mouth opened and closed a few times while he tried to blink away his confusion. "And an alternate dimension seemed like the best catchall?"

"Look, this is what we know about it." Nickie counted on her fingers. "The coins help us teleport in and out of the Clubhouse. Everything we have on us, whatever we're carrying, comes with us, too. It's the only place we've found where I didn't hear the Gorafrex's drumbeat inside my *head* when it was trying to magic or lure witches and wizards or shimmy out of its host to find a new one. And the three of us are the only people who can get in and out of there."

"Well, except for the Gorafrex, now," Laura added. "For some reason."

"Oh, yeah. For some reason." Ronan puffed out a sigh through loose lips and dragged the basket of nachos away from Tiberius to cram a few more into his mouth. "You Hadstroms sure do seem to fall into things, don't you?"

Laura folded her arms and looked genuinely insulted. "I like to think of it as a combination of skill and dedication."

"Plus, a little luck," Nickie added. "Sometimes."

"Yeah, maybe."

"Well, now would be the perfect time for a lot more luck to fall right into your laps." Ronan pushed himself away from the table and stepped back over the bench. "Finish your drinks. We're going on a little side trip."

The Hadstrom sisters looked at each other, but no one else moved from the table.

"Where, exactly?" Nickie asked.

"Hey, don't get me wrong. I like a little luck every now and then." Ronan thumped his fellow Huldu on the back and nodded for Tiberius to get to his feet. "But with something like this, trusting to luck seems like a rookie mistake, whether or not skill and dedication have anything to do with it."

"That's not what she asked," Nathan said.

"Listen, I don't have or want any problem with you, Kashgar—"

"Part Kashgar."

"Yeah, okay. We're gonna go have a little chat with the one magical who seems to know more about this than any of us put together. Back to the beginning, right?"

"Which is?"

The orange-bearded Huldu glanced at Emily and grimaced. "The last Velikan sounds like a good place to start. Again. Let's go. We'll wait for you out front. Five minutes."

Ronan and Tiberius both brushed a surprising amount of nacho crumbs off the front of their overalls then disappeared back through the Mean-Eyed Cat, headed for the street out front.

Nickie raised her eyebrows and couldn't help a little smile. "Guess I won't be the only one who hasn't met Rutilda anymore. That's a plus."

"Canceled out by the fact that we're going to talk to her with a couple of gnomes." Emily stared daggers through the inside of the bar, despite that both Huldus were gone. "I seriously doubt they'll make it as chaperones."

"Not chaperones, Em." Laura lifted her legs over the bench and readjusted her purse on her shoulder. "They want to know what's going on as much as we do. And how to get magic working again as soon as possible."

"You think they can help get the Gorafrex out of the Clubhouse and into its prison?" Nickie reached out for a nacho and tossed it in her mouth. "You know, the one that was built to hold it."

"I have no clue. But the mechanics have been taking care of this ship since the beginning, so what's the worst that could happen?"

Emily drained the rest of her beer then stared at her oldest sister. "Famous last words, Laura."

"Okay, Em. You don't have to be happy about it, and I'm not even asking you to smile. But maybe take the prickly down a notch. Please."

With a sigh, Emily plastered a severely fake grin on her face and shot Laura two thumbs-up.

"Work in progress. You'll get there."

CHAPTER TWENTY-THREE

Ronan and Tiberius were waiting for them on the sidewalk in front of the Mean-Eyed Cat. The taller, perpetually squinting Huldu had his hands thrust so far down in the pockets of his overalls that he hunched over a little. Ronan paced back and forth, tugging on his orange beard.

"Great. You took the full five minutes." He nodded at the witches and turned in a tight circle. "We'd offer everybody a ride to the museum, but we can't really rely on our usual means of transportation. Especially with non-Huldus."

"What are your usual means of transportation?" Nickie asked.

"Tunneling. Slipping underground." Ronan shrugged. "That's as technical as I'm willing to get right now."

Emily smirked. "Does it involve glowing blue tree roots?"

"What?"

"Probably not. Never mind."

"So, it's time to carpool," Tiberius muttered. "Who's volunteering?"

Laura turned around to eye the back of the Mean-Eyed Cat and the parking lot. "Okay, follow me."

She headed toward the back with the rest of the group on her heels. When she stopped behind the dumpster at the back of the parking lot, she got a bunch of confused looks and a lot more Huldu suspicion.

"Unless you're about to tell me this dumpster has wheels and goes faster than an actual car, I don't know what we're doing here." Ronan sniffed, flared his nostrils, and stepped away from the dumpster. "Please tell me that's not your car."

"Definitely not." Laura held out both her hands toward her sisters and nodded. "But I thought it might be a good idea to show some new Huldu friends that we still have a few tricks up our sleeves. 'Cause both of you seem a little cynical."

Tiberius snorted. "I mean, you see why, don't you?"

Emily slapped Laura's palm before squeezing her sister's hand. "And you're about to see why you should have a little more faith in the Hadstrom sisters."

Nickie let out a little laugh and grabbed Laura's other hand. "We're doing this in front of Huldus. Never thought I'd say that."

Laura shot Nathan and Chuck a reassuring smile. "Come a little closer, guys. Unless you wanna be left behind."

They reluctantly shuffled forward until the whole group formed a nice, cozy little circle.

"We just had a conversation about the fact that *magic*

doesn't work." Ronan blinked up at the witches with wide eyes. "Is it messing with your brains too?"

The Hadstrom sisters ignored him, and Nickie lifted her hand into the middle of the circle. The black legacy ring on her thumb flashed with a muted light, then the pearly, opalescent bubble appeared on her ring. It grew quickly and easily without sputtering or shrinking again, and she grinned.

"What am I seeing right now?" Ronan dragged a hand down the side of his face and tugged on his beard again. "I mean, I know what a transport bubble is, but how…"

"We'll chalk it all up to our last name. How 'bout that?" Laura nodded at the gnome before the transport bubble grew large enough between them that they couldn't see each other through the shimmering membrane of Nickie's spell.

"Wait." Chuck let out an excited laugh. "I get to ride in one of these things?"

"You're part of the whole thing, aren't you, Peabrain?" Ronan nodded and stepped into the bubble. "Can't back out now."

Everyone else stepped through the mostly clear membrane after him. Laura had barely enough time to shout, "Think about going under the museum."

Then the bubble disappeared from behind the dumpster, and no one in or around the Mean-Eyed Cat noticed Austin's new Queen of Blues disappear with her sisters, a Peabrain, a tall part Kashgar, and two much shorter Huldus.

When the bubble burst, it dropped all seven of its passengers in the darkness of the unlit parking lot behind the history museum downtown. They all knocked against each other a little after having been crammed together in the same transport spell. Emily rubbed her forehead and stumbled backward. "Hey, no headbutting. That's definitely off-limits."

"If I ran my head into yours on purpose, witch, you'd know the difference. Trust me." Tiberius shot his arms out to his sides to steady himself and looked for a minute like he was trying to flap some wings and fly away.

"Okay. This isn't exactly *under* the museum, but we're close."

Chuck shot Laura a sheepish smile. "Sorry. That was probably me. First time. Plus, I've never been *under* a museum before, so..."

"Don't worry about it, Chuck." Laura patted his shoulder, then stepped around the recovering magicals and waved them after her. "This way. We're looking for a manhole cover."

"Wow." Ronan made a face, then shook his head. "You know, I was really hoping the Engineer hadn't built some kinda nest for herself in the sewer, but I'm not surprised."

"She doesn't live in the sewer." Laura turned around and shot the orange-bearded Huldu a disapproving frown. "That's the only entrance I know of to get down to her... Well, it's not actually a house, really. To where she lives, anyway. Last time I was here, I had to climb down through the manhole. Follow my lead."

"Oh, sure. Like how you took your sisters' hands and were suddenly able to cast a transport bubble, huh?"

Tiberius stepped away from his Huldu friend. "I'm not

holding your hand, Ronan. Not even for a little extra magic."

"Nobody asked you to, T."

"Speaking of gnomes and magic…" Nickie jogged a little to catch up to the Huldus walking beside Laura. "How did you manage to cast any at all?"

"Is this a trick question?" Ronan scowled at her over his shoulder. "You lit a famous person's guitar on fire just by playing it."

"No." She lowered her voice. "I mean the spell on the humans at the bar. The ones who wanted to forget."

"You don't have to whisper, Nickie," Emily called from a few yards behind them. "I can still hear you, and I already know what they did to those people."

"Oh. That." Ronan turned again to look Emily up and down, then shrugged and kept walking to the history museum's back wall. "Believe it or not, we Huldus have a pretty comprehensive library of some of the more powerful techniques that tend to work a lot better than regular magic, especially when stuff like this—"

"Potions," Tiberius grumbled. "We made some potions, and they help us do our jobs when we can't really depend on magic to do what it's been doing for as long as any of us have been alive. And we've been around a lot longer than you witches, believe me."

"I don't think anyone's gonna argue with you on that," Nickie muttered.

"Good. You'd lose."

"Wait a minute." Emily walked a little faster to catch up. "Did I hear a Huldu say something about potions?"

"They're pretty complicated." Tiberius gave the

youngest Hadstrom sister a dismissive wave. "I'm not gonna bore you with all the details or waste both our time trying to explain to you how it works."

"What about the Tenebantur?" Emily asked. "You know how *that* works?"

Both gnomes stopped short and whirled around to find the youngest Hadstrom sister grinning at them, her hands on her hips.

Ronan's eye twitched. "Did she just say what I thought she said?"

"Yep." Tiberius tipped his head back and gave Emily another glance up and down. "Maybe she's smarter than she looks."

"Actually, my little sister's a whiz with potions." Nickie nodded at the gnomes as she passed them to join Laura beside the manhole cover. "You might learn a thing or two from her, as long as you don't mind asking a *witch* to share a little knowledge."

"Hey, I have nothing against witches, okay?" Tiberius shoved his hands back into the pockets of his overalls and squinted even more deeply at Emily. "Only this one. She's been givin' me the death stare since we met."

Emily passed the gnomes too and leaned toward Tiberius a little to mutter, "The Tenebantur, buddy. Stick *that* in your pipe."

"Okay, first, that would be the dumbest, most deadly thing anyone's ever done. Probably. And second, I don't have a pipe. So there."

Chuck snorted as he and Nathan walked past the shocked Huldus in the parking lot.

Tiberius shook his head. "Keep laughing, Peabrain. You're not even supposed to be here."

"I know, right?"

The rest of the group stopped with Laura in front of the single manhole in the museum's parking lot beside the back wall. Nathan cocked his head. "This is the entrance to the Velikan's…what? Lair?"

"For anyone who's trying to get down there from the surface, yeah." Laura reached out toward the manhole cover without thinking. When her silver legacy ring didn't flash and no spell burst from her hand to knock the thick metal disk aside, she dropped her hand against her thigh and sighed. "Right. No magic for that."

"I got it." Nathan knelt beside the manhole and hooked his finger through the vent holes in the metal cover. He managed to pop the thing a few inches out of the hole and dragged it aside before something loud and clearly huge rumbled beneath the parking lot. He dropped the metal cover with a clang. "What was that?"

"Probably the Engineer pacing around down there," Ronan suggested, "waiting for magic to come back like the rest of us."

"Have you seen her before?" Laura asked. "I mean, up close?"

"No, but I was knee-deep in the mess she left behind last week."

The oldest Hadstrom sister shook her head and gazed at the small opening in the cover. "She's not big enough to make that kinda noise."

"All right, then, Miss Know It All." Ronan spread his

arms. "If you know everything about this last Engineer friend of yours, go ahead and—"

The ground trembled beneath them, then another loud rumble rose from beneath the parking lot. That rumble ended in an earsplitting crack, and then the group of magicals and Chuck were tossed all over the place. Nathan fell back away from the manhole. Tiberius tripped over his own feet and knocked himself over sideways. Nickie stumbled backward into Chuck, who caught her around the waist and made her cry out in pain from her bruised ribs.

"Got an explanation for this?" Ronan shouted.

"Not…exactly." Laura's hands slammed against the asphalt as she caught herself from falling flat on her face, and she staggered a little before regaining her balance.

"That doesn't mean we don't have a solution." Emily wobbled across the trembling ground toward Laura and grabbed her sister's shoulder. "I didn't think to bring any potions with me to work, so I'm fresh out. Sorry."

"Not your fault, Em. And neither is this earthquake."

"Yeah, I wouldn't say *that's* my fault, either. But if we can do something about it, we should. Right?" Emily pointed at the top of the museum. The flagpole at the very top broke free of its base and toppled over the side of the building. Right where it had been, a column of flashing silver light burst from the roof of the history museum, illuminating the Austin skyline like a giant spotlight.

"I'm with you there, Em. That doesn't look good at all. Nickie?"

"Coming." Nickie stumbled toward them, holding her ribs. Chuck stared at her in concern before another trembling wave rocked the parking lot. He turned his attention to not falling backward onto the asphalt.

"So, you have no idea what that is?" Ronan asked.

"It looked like a geyser of magic that appeared out of nowhere and is now tearing the history museum apart." Emily clasped Nickie's outstretched hand and tried to keep both of them on their feet. "If I had to guess."

"Probably an accurate assessment. Hey, T, did you bring—"

"Nope! Didn't bring any potions for this kinda disaster, man." Tiberius struggled to get back up on his feet. "So, I'm out of ideas here."

"We're not." Laura raised her free hand and nodded at Nickie to do the same. "Shutting off the geyser so we keep the museum from demolishing itself, yeah?"

"Sure. Why not?"

Together, the two oldest Hadstrom sisters—each clutching one of Emily's hands—reached toward the crumbling museum. All three legacy rings flashed, and a wave of yellow light four feet wide shot up from the sisters' hands toward the self-destructing roof. It hit the column of magic shooting up from the building's center and seemed to calm it down a little. The leaking magic dimmed and sputtered, then slowly started to withdraw back inside the museum.

"Keep going!" Laura shouted.

Both Huldus' jaws dropped as they watched the Hadstrom witches using their magic when magic didn't work for anyone. Ever. Tiberius slapped a hand to his forehead and blinked.

Emily gripped her sisters' fingers even tighter and

could only offer her magical backup plus a little encouragement. "It's almost gone. So, I think it's working."

Nickie laughed through gritted teeth against the constant force of magic flowing in that wave from her and Laura's outstretched hands. "You make a good cheerleader, Em."

"No way am I wearing one of those uniforms, though."

"Would ya look at that?" Ronan tugged on his orange beard and let out a chuckle of disbelief. "These witches might have a chance—"

The ground bucked again in another, much larger shockwave barreling beneath the parking lot. A giant fissure ripped all the way from the bottom of the history museum to the top, filling the air with one more deafening crack as the building all but completely split apart. Two trees groaned and snapped behind them, and the cars parked along the street in front of the museum launched into a series of activated alarms blaring through the night. The asphalt beneath the Hadstrom sisters jerked sideways and buckled, then smashed back together and knocked the witches apart. Laura stumbled sideways, and the spell sputtered out as soon as her fingers were pulled out of Emily's.

"Wait!" Nickie shouted, then she and Emily were both knocked in the other direction.

The leaking geyser of magic burst back out of the top of the museum as if the Hadstrom sisters hadn't done a thing to stop it.

Ronan glanced from Laura to the collapsing museum and back again. "Aw, screw it."

The orange-bearded Huldu lunged toward Laura across the rupturing parking lot and clamped a hand down on her wrist. Her silver ring flashed on her thumb, and when Ronan lifted his hand toward the museum, a stream of neon-green bubbles burst from his fingers.

"Ha! That's what I'm talking about!" His wide eyes glimmered with green light, and he swirled his hand in a large circle, directing the spell he hadn't completely believed he could cast. "Okay, T. I'm not saying you have to hold my hand or anything, but this is actually working..."

"I'm...working on it." Tiberius was having a hard time trying to half crawl, half stumble toward his fellow gnome while the ground kept tossing him around like a marble in a shoebox. Finally, he leapt toward Ronan like sliding into home plate. His outstretched hand missed Ronan's completely, but he clamped down around the other gnome's ankle and held on tight.

More green bubbles burst from Tiberius' hand, and together, the Huldus powered by Laura's magic and her legacy ring herded the spraying geyser of untamed magic back down into the hole on the history museum's roof.

"Only a guess, here, but I'm thinking this would be a lot easier if we had all three of you." Ronan jerked his head toward Emily and Nickie, who'd almost gotten back on their feet. "Whenever's good for—"

Something beneath the parking lot cracked and dropped, sending the witches, the gnomes, Chuck, and Nathan slumping sideways to the left. Nickie and Emily slid down the declining asphalt toward Laura and managed to grab onto their sister's legs.

"Ow! Really?" All three legacy rings flashed together with a brighter burst than any of them had seen so far, and warm, tingling energy surged across the line of connected Hadstrom witches and their new Huldu friends.

"Hold it!" Tiberius slammed his free palm down on the slanted asphalt and let out a shout of concentration and effort. The parking lot glowed bright pink, and the incline jerked back up to settle into something mostly flat. Once everyone could stand straight again without worrying about sliding sideways down Austin, both gnomes turned their attention and their Hadstrom-powered magic to the museum itself. An eight-foot section of the back wall had already separated from the rest of the building and was in the time-sensitive process of toppling sideways like a flimsy cutout of a movie set.

The Huldus' green bubbles blinked into shimmering white and tripled in size. Tiberius and Ronan both waved their arms around like they were directing some massive, unheard orchestra in the air. The bubbles burst against the falling wall and pushed everything back up into place. More bubbles settled into a protective casing around the entire museum, packing in tighter and tighter until there wasn't an inch of space between any of them. The museum cracked and groaned, smashing violently back into place as if every crumbling piece was a dislocated joint being reset by two gnomes.

When the bubbles burst and the gnomes lowered their hands, the only sound came from the blaring alarms on the cars parked out front. Tiberius snapped his fingers, and the alarms cut out instantly.

Lying on her side on the asphalt, Emily puffed out a sigh and released her death-grip on Laura's ankle. Tiberius groaned, let go of Ronan's leg, and rolled over onto his back. "This keeps getting better, doesn't it?"

"Ha!" Ronan released Laura, gave her an excited little pat on the back, and slapped the top of his head repeatedly with both hands. "Boy, a week without any real magic feels like a lifetime. Whatever you witches are eating to drum up that kinda horsepower, I want some!"

Nickie sat back on the asphalt, still holding her side with a grimace, and pointed at Emily. "She's the chef."

"Chef *and* potions, eh?" Ronan winked at the youngest Hadstrom sister. "You and I need to chat later."

Emily smoothed the hair away from her face and stared at the perfectly restored history museum. "I have a few conditions for that, but sure."

CHAPTER TWENTY-FOUR

"Nice. We can hash out the details whenever. Now." Ronan clapped his hands together, rubbed them, and stared at the gaping manhole in front of them. In the magic-induced earthquake, the metal cover had popped off and now lay a few yards away—what had previously been downhill in the slanted parking lot. "Ready to go ask that Engineer what the heck kinda prank she was trying to pull down there?"

"Wait! Uh...can I get a little help over here, first?"

The Huldus and Hadstrom witches turned to see Chuck tangled up in one of the trees that had snapped in the earthquake. He was lying on his side, propping his head up in one hand, his legs and lower back covered by leafy branches.

"Forgot about those." Ronan clapped a hand down on Laura's shoulder and reached toward Chuck. A yellow bubble shot from his hand and hurtled toward the trapped human before wrapping around him. The tree lifted a few feet and smashed back down to the asphalt after the bubble yanked a shrieking Chuck across the parking lot toward the manhole.

"Hey." Laura shrugged Ronan's hand off her shoulder. The bubble burst and dropped Chuck from three feet above the ground. He landed with a thud and a heavy grunt. "Sorry, Chuck."

He pulled his knees up to his chest and wheezed, "I'm good."

She turned back toward the orange-bearded gnome. "Look, we definitely appreciate your help with this almost-destroyed-museum issue, but let me be perfectly clear. My sisters and I are *not* an extra battery you can carry around and tap into whenever you—"

Tiberius slapped her shoe and sent an instantly conjured orb of bright white light shooting down into the manhole.

Laura glared down at him. "…feel like it."

"Whoops." Tiberius blinked and jerked his hand away from her foot. "My bad. Couldn't help it."

"Well, you're gonna have to help it, okay? And we need you to keep our magical power boost quiet for now. Think you can do that?"

"Hmm. I guess it depends." Tiberius scratched the side of his face and looked Laura up and down. "How much would you charge a few Huldus to tap into that—"

"*What?*"

"He's kidding." Ronan wrapped his fists around the back of Tiberius' overall straps and jerked the taller Huldu to his feet. "Of course, he's kidding. Not funny, T. Keep the bad jokes to a minimum until we're done with the Velikan down there. Got it?"

Tiberius brushed his friend off and readjusted his overalls. "Yeah, yeah. Just think about the offer, okay?"

Laura folded her arms and glared at him. "Maybe you should go down first. Before I push you."

"Ooh…" The squinty gnome let out a little chuckle, waved her off, and stepped down into the manhole after the orb of light. His boots found the first metal rung, and he started his descent, still chuckling to himself.

After helping Chuck up off the ground, Nickie walked with him toward the open manhole. Emily watched them and couldn't contain a laugh. "You guys really are a good match. You okay?"

Nickie gritted her teeth, holding her side again while Chuck limped forward, rubbing his tailbone. "We'll be fine, Em. Thanks."

"Hey, where's Nathan?" Laura turned in a slow circle around the parking lot, scanning the darkness pierced only a little by the streetlights in front of the museum. "Nathan?"

"He was just here." Emily gestured toward the asphalt in front of the manhole, and her mouth dropped open. "You don't think he—"

Ronan was already fully submerged and climbing down the rebar ladder after Tiberius. He gazed up at the three witches and Chuck peering down into the hole after him, then glanced down to shout, "What?"

"We're looking for Nathan," Laura offered.

"Shh! Hold on." The gnome cupped a hand around his

ear, then let out a barking laugh. "Looks like Tiberius found a Kashgar hanging out underground and waiting for someone to find him. Huh. That sounds more like a Huldu, but—"

"Ronan."

"Oh, yeah. Your part-Kashgar's down there, all right. T's keeping him company 'til we all finish climbing down, okay? Keep your pants on. Yeesh." Shaking his head and chuckling, Ronan quickly climbed down rung after rung.

Back above the manhole, Emily covered her mouth and couldn't keep her snigger from escaping. "Yeah, Laura. Keep your pants on."

Laura shot her sister a warning glance, then shook her head and lowered herself feet-first into the manhole. "I can't believe none of us noticed Nathan falling right into this hole."

"Did he, though?" Nickie gestured for Emily to follow behind Laura. "He stepped away when the earthquake started."

"Well, whatever happened," Laura shouted as she made her way down the ladder, "he better be okay. And Rutilda better have a good explanation for unleashing the magical version of Old Faithful right up through the museum."

Emily chuckled and grinned up at Nickie and Chuck, watching her from above. "She's in a joking mood now, isn't she?"

Nickie didn't answer but turned around, gave Chuck a quick peck on the cheek, and climbed down after her sisters. "Welcome to the magical side of Austin, babe."

"You know, despite being tossed around and knowing

the kinda bruises I'm gonna see tomorrow, it's a lot more fun than I expected."

"I'm glad you're enjoying yourself." Nickie's laugh was cut short by a sharp, hissing breath through her teeth. *I might be, too, if my ribs would quit screaming at me for longer than a few minutes.*

When the entire group had climbed down the rebar ladder, they found Nathan sitting cross-legged in the middle of the stone passageway leading to the Velikan Engineer's lair beneath the history museum. He stood, dusted off his hands, and shrugged under Tiberius' orb of light bobbing beneath the tunnel's ceiling. "I'm glad you guys finally decided to show up."

"What happened?" Laura rushed toward him and looked him over in the dim light. "Are you okay?"

"I'm fine. Which is pretty weird." Nathan wrapped his arms around Laura, who'd melted against him for a relieved hug, and glanced up at the dark ceiling of the tunnel. "Since I pretty much fell right through the parking lot."

"You what?" Laura pulled away from him with wide eyes.

"Yeah. When the earthquake tipped everything over. The ground opened up, I fell right in, and then this guy shot a light at me." When he stuck his thumb out toward Tiberius, the squinty gnome mimed tipping a hat to the Hadstrom witches.

"Can't say I knew he was down here. But hey, good thing I tapped into that portable Hadstrom-witch battery, right?"

"We're not having that conversation," Laura told the

gnome. She released Nathan, patted his chest, then turned and headed down the shallowly declining tunnel stretching in front of them. "Let's go find Rutilda."

"Battery?" Nathan glanced down at Tiberius, who shrugged and headed after Laura.

Emily, Nickie, and Ronan followed, and Chuck stepped up beside Nathan to give the physics professor a sympathetic slap on the back. "Apparently, if the girls make a magical chain with two gnomes, it stops earthquakes and puts everything back together again. Pretty cool, right?"

Nathan snorted and headed with a grinning Chuck down the passage.

Laura didn't have any trouble remembering the route through what quickly became a maze of branching passageways, followed by overlapping walkways of metal grates. She led the group right to the edge of the long, narrow catwalk branching across the massive chasm with no end in sight. "This is it."

"Woah." Emily stared at the sudden drop on either side of the catwalk and the platform where all seven of them now stood. The catwalk led to another massive platform on the other side of the cavern with a thick metal column rising all the way to the cavern's ceiling. A handful of other large platforms were connected by various other grated walkways, some with railings, some without.

"So, where's this Engineer?" Ronan tugged on his beard and reached out to grab the back of Tiberius' overalls when the taller Huldu leaned dangerously far over the edge of their current platform.

"She was right on the other side of this catwalk," Laura said, trying to peer through the netting reaching up from either side of the catwalk and still somehow connected to the cavern's ceiling. The Velikan's lair was completely silent, and the first wave of doubt washed over the oldest Hadstrom sister. "Something's wrong."

"You mean besides the fact that she tried to bring that museum down around her?" Ronan stepped toward the catwalk and shook his head. "Do you have any idea how much paperwork and bureaucratic crapola comes with a magically eradicated landmark? Even worse if it's part of everyday Peabrain life, which that museum clearly is. Doesn't even matter that most of the history's wrong, anyway."

The orange-bearded gnome scoffed and kept muttering about all the extra work ahead of him as he walked across the catwalk toward the platform on the opposite side. Tiberius followed closely behind, not bothering to steady himself with the rope netting but strutting along with his hands behind his back.

Laura took a deep breath and glanced at her sisters. "I'm serious, though. I can't put my finger on it, but something's different."

"Okay." Nickie nodded. "We'll keep our eyes open. No problem."

"All right." Laura turned around and followed the orb of light bobbing ahead of the two Huldu crossing the catwalk.

Before she was halfway across, she realized what had been giving her such a bad feeling. Half of the far platform had crumbled away from the rest, leaving a scattered jumble of all the junk Rutilda the Engineer had kept around her in her underground home. One of the other mesh walkways connecting that large center platform to another on the right was twisted and crumpled, obviously useless now for getting to the smaller platform. And there was a huge hole blasted through the center of the large metal column.

By the time the Hadstrom sisters, Chuck, and Nathan had reached the main platform, both Huldus were already busy digging through the Engineer's eclectically chaotic array of belongings.

"Look at this stuff." Tiberius jerked a thick black tarp off a pile of latched metal boxes and sent a wave of thick dust swirling all around him. He fell into a violent fit of coughing and frantically waved his arms around in front of his face. "Seriously lacking in responsible upkeep."

Something skittered across the platform, and Ronan whirled around, lifted his foot in hesitation. "What was that?"

"One of the giant cockroaches, if I had to guess." Laura gazed around the half-fallen platform and frowned.

"Giant *cockroaches*?"

"Yeah. She was eating them when I came down here to meet with her."

The orange-bearded gnome made a face and fiercely shook his head. "Nasty. You know, we had a theory the Engineer was losing her mind, but I'm pretty sure that makes it official."

"So, where is she?" Nickie asked.

"I don't know. Rutilda?" Laura gingerly stepped through the toppled crates and scattered piles of extra netting and tarps and a few random industrial nails.

"Maybe she's sleeping," Emily offered. "Grandma Eloise slept for days right before she passed."

"Em, I don't know if we can compare Grandma Eloise to a Velikan Engineer. Although I'm sure she'd probably be quite flattered by it, anyway." Laura swept aside a thick curtain of more netting, but it was covering more stone wall on the other side of the platform. "Besides, Rutilda told me she could hear me all the way up on the surface. Kinda hard to believe that she'd be able to sleep through that earthquake, our magic, and all seven of us stomping our way down here."

"Hey, I don't *stomp*."

Ronan elbowed Tiberius in the ribs and cocked his head. "You stomp."

Laura gazed up at the huge, jagged, charred hole in the metal column and frowned. Her next step crunched on something that sounded a little like glass, and she quickly pulled her foot away. When she stepped back, she recognized Rutilda's huge, metal-rimmed goggles with the ridiculously thick lenses that had made the Velikan Engineer's eyes so comically large. They were lying there, discarded, but then Laura recognized the Engineer's dark green jumpsuit mottled with patches of different-colored material. She would have thought she'd stumbled upon a sleeping Rutilda if it weren't for the fact that the Velikan's jumpsuit, socks, and massive boots were completely empty.

"Oh, no."

"Laura?"

The oldest Hadstrom sister stepped back again and called to the Huldus, "Does anyone know what happens to a Velikan when they die?"

"Huh. It's pretty violent, most of the time." Ronan tugged on his beard and walked around the giant metal column in the center of the platform toward her. "Kinda like a massive explosion of life energy and the rest of their magic. Tears things apart, and then the Velikan's body fizzles apart to drift away on the—oh."

"Yeah. I think I found the last Engineer."

CHAPTER TWENTY-FIVE

Laura frowned down at Rutilda's empty jumpsuit as the rest of their group gathered around the Velikan-shaped remains on the platform. "And I bet the magic that almost blew up the museum was hers, too."

Ronan pointed at the charred hole in the metal column and raised his eyebrows. "Oh, yeah. Look at that. Like she sent it all right up through there before…poof."

"She'd probably appreciate something a little less informal than *poof*, don't you think?"

"My bad. Before she released her life force back into the collective consciousness of the ship." The gnome spread his arms and leaned forward. "Better?"

"Sure."

Nickie stopped beside her sister and folded her arms. "I was really looking forward to meeting her. You guys got to."

"And she was really helpful." Emily sniffed and wiped at her nose, but she managed to blink back the tears before they ever had a chance to well up. "She laughed at my bad jokes."

"Always the measure of a good person." Chuck set a consoling hand on the youngest witch's shoulder.

"I know, right?"

"Great! Just great." Tiberius flung his hands in the air and smacked them back down against his thighs, turning in a tight circle. "We came down here to get some answers, and we're five minutes late. Guess we should resign ourselves to the fact that magic's never coming back for any of us but the three of you." He tossed his hand toward the Hadstrom sisters.

"Okay, T." Ronan shot the witches an exasperated look and went to comfort his buddy. "It's not the end of the world. You know that. Things are gonna get back on track soon. Probably. I mean, hey, a whole week with no dependable magic, but *we* got to tap into some up there in the parking lot, right? Just gotta be patient."

"And let us clean up our mess," Laura added. "We *will* fix this."

"Yeah." Nickie nodded and put her arm around Laura's shoulder. "We're Hadstroms. It's kind of what we were born to do."

"Aw, man." Emily sighed and hung her head. "I never got the chance to thank Rutilda for her help. She was the one who recommended I try potions in the first place."

"Well, yeah. The Engineers would know about that, too." Ronan cleared his throat. "Not that the Velikan ever really dabbled in potions. Too hands-on for them, I think."

"Serious bummer." Emily scratched the side of her head and lowered herself onto a stack of metal crates behind her. Something slid off the back of the crate and crashed to the platform with a startling clang. She leapt to her feet and spun around to see a huge sheet of metal teetering on the edge of the platform. Before she could think about reaching out to stop it, the metal sheet expanded, doubled in size, and started unfolding itself over and over like a rug being unrolled. Only in this case, the metal sheet unrolled itself into a steel staircase that held itself up without any support and just kept toppling over and over until the steps disappeared into the darkness of the chasm below them.

"Emily? What was that?"

"A total accident." The youngest Hadstrom sister pressed her hands on the stacked metal crates and leaned forward. The edge of the staircase had clamped itself onto the edge of the platform and didn't budge. "But I might've made us some stairs—"

Two thick, sturdy railings ejected from each side of the staircase with a bang. Emily jumped backward in surprise, then stepped around the boxes until she stood at the top of the metal stairs leading down into who knew what.

Blue and green lights flared to life along both railings and moved quickly down the staircase into the darkness. Then another round of lights flashed and moved down in the same pattern. "This remind you guys of something?"

Laura joined her sister at the edge of the stairs. "Flashing like all those trees this morning."

"Yeah, that's what I was thinking."

"What about the trees?" Ronan stalked toward the sisters and the edge of the staircase and studied it with a marginally curious frown. "That a witch thing or something?"

"Today, I guess it is." Laura pointed at the large, thickly etched symbol on the very first metal step. "What's that?"

"Woah." Emily cocked her head. "That kinda looks like the same symbols in the watchtower."

Ronan tugged on his beard again and turned away from them, shaking his head. "I'm never gonna understand half the stuff they're talking about."

"Nathan?"

"Yeah."

Emily pointed at the symbol in the metal. "Can you read that?"

"Yep. Same symbol for the Isolation Vein."

Laura turned around to search his gaze. "*This* is the symbol you found down there?"

Nathan nodded. "Kashgar runes. Definitely."

"Wow."

"Isolation Vein." Nickie nodded slowly and folded her arms. "Sounds like that staircase has as much for the Hadstrom witches as the watchtower did."

"You guys wanna walk down a set of stairs that unfolded into a bottomless pit?" Chuck swallowed thickly and grabbed Nickie's hand, pulling her a little farther away from the edge of the platform. "No questions asked?"

"At this point, Chuck, we don't really have a lot of other options." Laura glanced at her sisters and nodded. "Ready?"

"Yep."

"Hey, wait a minute." Chuck pulled Nickie completely aside this time. "What if something happens? You know, completely unstable staircase. Crumbling Velikan...whatever this is? Another earthquake?"

"Okay, okay, slow down, Peabrain." Tiberius shuffled

toward them with his hands in his pockets and squinted at the Hadstrom sisters. "Nothing like a little bit of luck, right? And maybe a few Huldus who actually wanna see the three of you fix this mess so we can all move on."

He pulled three large, teardrop-shaped vials from the pockets of his overalls and handed them out to the witches.

"What are these?" Laura reached out for her vial and turned it over in her hand.

"Teleporting potions." Tiberius shrugged. "Granted, they're grounded to the closest Huldu cafeteria, but at least they'll take you away from wherever you absolutely don't want to be anymore. That's all I got."

"Huh." Emily took her vial and inspected it. "That'll do. Thanks."

"Aw, look at you." Ronan clapped a hand on his buddy's shoulder and shook the taller gnome. "Crawling out of your comfort zone and making new friends, T."

"Hardly."

Emily rolled her eyes. "Yeah, don't push it."

"Well, I have no problem calling you guys friends." Nickie nodded at the gnomes and pocketed her teleporting potion as well. "Even though you did crash my show."

Ronan pointed at her. "You were on fire, kid. Literally and figuratively. So, don't quit. Maybe don't play any hardcore gigs until magic starts following its rules, huh?"

"I'll see what I can do."

"All right, Peabrain. Kashgar." Ronan stepped away and waved Chuck and Nathan toward him.

Nathan drew a deep breath and shot Laura an irritated glance. "I think I'm gonna stop correcting people about that."

"Well, *we* know who you are." She stepped toward him for a quick hug. "Guess we'll have to take a raincheck for a date without any magical interruptions, huh?"

"I'll put it on the list with all the times I'm not letting Chuck pay for our drinks." Nathan winked at her, released her, and nodded toward the staircase down into darkness. "Good luck with whatever's at the bottom of that."

"Thanks."

"Wait, where are *we* going?" Chuck looked up at Nathan and blinked. "I mean, don't get me wrong, I don't think anyone could get me to go down *there*. But…well, shouldn't we wait for them to come back?"

"Probably not, babe." Nickie grabbed his face with both hands and gave him a short, fierce kiss. "But I'll call you when we're done, okay?"

"I get it. We're back to that now, huh?" Chuck ran a hand through his blond hair and let out a dry, airy laugh. "Okay, then. I'll go hang out with Speed until then."

"Yeah, he could use some company."

"The train's leaving, kids." Ronan overexaggerated another wave and pointed at Tiberius, who was already halfway across the catwalk back up toward the tunnels and their return to the surface. "Let's get a move on. And good luck, witches. Plus, some extra skill and dedication, if that's what works for ya. If things don't work out the way you plan, you'll be seeing our beautiful Huldu mugs again in the next few days, so… It's up to you."

"Point taken." Nickie shot the gnome a thumbs up and blew Chuck a kiss before he turned to follow Nathan and Ronan back across the catwalk. Then she turned back toward the unfolded metal staircase and took a deep breath. "Well. One more adventure underground, right?"

"Yeah, I hope we find something cool."

Laura chuckled and stepped onto the first metal step. She grabbed the railings on both sides and shook them a little, testing the stability. The stairs didn't budge. "Let's hope we find something *helpful*, Em. As fun as I'm sure this is gonna be, we need answers."

"Hey, answers can be cool, too." Emily grinned. "So is this."

CHAPTER TWENTY-SIX

The blue and green lights flashing down both metal railings gave the Hadstrom sisters enough light to see the next few steps in front of them as they cautiously made their way down into the darkness. Emily gazed around at the complete blackness everywhere, punctured by green and blue. "This is kinda weird, right? Like, the only thing that exists is this staircase."

"Something tells me that's kind of the point, Em." Nickie stepped carefully behind Laura, still feeling like if she moved too quickly or brought her foot down too hard, she'd fall right through the metal sheets. "I don't think this thing would've appeared anywhere else. I mean, what are the odds that right after the last Velikan kicks the bucket, these stairs spill down into a giant hole, start flashing like the trees that saved us, *and* have the same runes from the Isolation Vein that our rings were made from?"

"Pretty small." Laura paused and lifted one hand off the railing to look at the flashing lights streaking down into the darkness. "Does it look like the lights are speeding up?

We've been walking down these things for so long, I can't really tell."

"Oh, yeah." Emily hummed in acknowledgment. "Probably a little faster."

"So, that either means something crazy's about to happen..." Nickie chuckled. "Or we're finally getting close to the bottom. Here's hoping for option number two."

"Yep. We're staying positive." Laura forced herself to loosen her grip on the railing and move a little faster. "Great calf workout, though."

Emily snorted.

"So, Laura..."

"So, Nickie..."

"While we're taking these stairs down into the middle of nowhere, wanna tell us more about what you saw at Astro's?"

Emily stopped on the stairs. "Astro's? When did you go to see *that* loon?"

Laura let out an aggravated sigh, although it was aimed more at the soothsayer and his vague ramblings with the scrying pool than her sister. "I don't know. Around six or so. Six-thirty. With Mom."

"Ha! *Mom* took you to see him, huh? Let me guess. You were trying to find out more about that Tenebantur potion because you didn't think Nickie and I knew enough about it. Even though we got a hair from the old man who actually *invented* the thing."

"It had nothing to do with me not trusting you guys, Em. How do you think I heard about the Tenebantur in the first place?"

"Uh...maybe you read it somewhere. I don't know."

Between them on the staircase, Nickie chuckled. "Laura gets her hands on a lot of weird, lost, old things. But I don't think a two-hundred-year-old banned potion is just laying around for anyone to find."

"Which was why I went to see the soothsayer," Laura added. "Because Leonidas was one of the magicals who'd used the Tenebantur with Astro that first time and recognized it when the Gorafrex started building the potion all by itself."

"The *fairy* Leonidas?" Emily blinked heavily into the darkness. "So, either he chickened out and wrote down the whole recipe for the Gorafrex, or…"

"It's the *or,* Em. Apparently, when it was spending so much time in the prison, the Gorafrex was able to pick up on different thoughts and events and information in the ether. Or at least, that's what Astro called it. And because the guy's a soothsayer and has used a scrying pool who knows how many times, the Tenebantur recipe… leaked out of his head, I guess. And the Gorafrex found it."

Emily burst out laughing, and the sound echoed like a jackhammer all around them. She clamped a hand over her mouth and stared into the darkness, waiting for the echo to die away. "That's kind of a ridiculous explanation. Don't you think?"

"I have to agree with you on that one, Em. But, it makes sense. And then Astro did this weird thing with the scrying pool and went into a trance."

"And you got a prophecy?" Nickie asked.

"I wouldn't call it that. More like a magical puppet show, maybe?" Laura chose to laugh instead of letting herself grow more frustrated by how much Astro's revelation still didn't make sense. "Something about the original Hadstroms, building the rings, the Gorafrex, and how they're all tied together in some way that nobody knew about the first time that thing got locked up. I don't know. I still haven't had a lot of time to think it through. But, Astro seemed to think he'd given me the answers for how to lock up the Gorafrex again, if I can ever dig it up out of all that total nonsense. So did Mom, actually."

"Huh. Well, if Mom thought it was important, I guess it has to be."

"Nickie, Mom's not part of the Hadstrom legacy. I mean, besides being our Mom."

"Yeah, but she does know Astro. And whether he's being serious about something, right?"

"I guess." Laura reached down for the next step and lost her balance when she stepped on level ground instead. "Woah. Hey! I think we reached the bottom."

"Cool." Emily peered around Nickie to see the blue and green flashing lights were blinking a lot faster now and still moved ahead of them down a narrow hallway stretching out from the bottom of the stairs. "Looks like the staircase was meant to be here, too."

"And we made it down without any problems." Laura turned to smile at both of her sisters, whose faces were intermittently lit by the blue and green lights flashing down the railings beneath their hands. "At this point, that kinda makes me think we're supposed to be here."

"Yeah, but now we have to wait for the next weird thing to happen. That's how it works, right?"

Nickie slid her foot out to double-check she'd reached the bottom then stopped beside Laura. "Or, Em, we could keep a positive attitude about the whole thing while we keep walking through the darkness who knows how far underground right now."

"I *am* being positive. Since when did you opt for boring?"

"Oh, I don't know. Since I can't even play a guitar without setting it on fire. Since the Huldus traced most, if not all, the magical mishaps in Austin back to us. Since everything in the last two weeks has added up to right now." Nickie ran a hand through her hair and let out a wry laugh. "I'm not thinking about it as boring, either, Em. It's more like I'm ready for some normal again, you know?"

"Can't argue with that." Emily reached the bottom of the stairs next, and the Hadstrom sisters peered into the darkness interspersed with blinking lights leading them farther down the tunnel. "I really hope we don't have to walk back *up* those stairs to get out of here, though."

Almost as if she'd said the magic password, the thick railings on either side of the suspended staircase jammed back down into the bottom of the stairs. Then the last step snapped and folded back up on itself. The sisters only saw a few of the silver stairs flashing and rolling back up in the blue and green light now running on either side of the tunnel, and then they couldn't see anything behind them but impenetrable darkness.

When the metallic clang of the folding stairs stopped echoing, Emily realized her mouth had fallen open. She shut it. "Maybe I spoke too soon."

"You can thank Tiberius for his potions later, Em. I'm sure he'll be totally thrilled to see us again when we use them to get us out of here."

Laura set a hand on Nickie's shoulder and nodded. "Yeah, *after* we find whatever answers we're supposed to find all the way at the bottom of a giant pit. So, let's go."

Emily snorted and carefully followed her sisters and the flashing lights along the floor. "How many times have you gone looking for things at the bottom of a giant pit, Dr. Archaeologist?"

"More times than I can count, Em."

"And would you rate this giant pit as better or worse than the countless others?"

Laura laughed softly, highly aware of the loud echo in this place, wherever it really was. "Not sure yet. I'll have to get back to you on that one."

Somewhere between five minutes and an hour later—it was impossible to tell the time down here, and the Hadstrom sisters' phones had all inexplicably died—the green and blue lights were now strobing along the walls of the tunnel. Laura paused when she noticed the lights stopped a few feet up ahead. "Okay, so that's either a dead end or something else we're gonna need a little magic to see. Be careful moving forward."

"Got it. I can do careful—" Emily tripped on an uneven patch of tunnel floor and choked on her laughter. "I'm good."

Reaching out with both hands in front of her, Laura slid her feet along the ground, searching for anything that might hit her hands and feet first instead of her face. But when she passed the point where the blue and green lights leading the way had stopped, she still felt empty air in front of her.

"Hands?" Laura reached out and waited to feel her sisters' fingers in hers. "Might be time for a little light."

"Yep." Nickie stepped up on her left.

Emily appeared on Laura's right in the darkness, and the Hadstrom sisters fumbled for each other's hands. The minute they were all touching, something huge clicked into place with an echoing slam. The space in front of them flared with a blinding light, and when it faded, the witches blinked furiously against the glare.

"Okay, Em." Still squinting, Laura took in the massive chamber in front of them and nodded. "Now I can answer your question. I'd say this is one of the top five coolest dark pits I've explored."

"Huh. I was expecting top three, at least."

CHAPTER TWENTY-SEVEN

They stood in the entrance to a massive circular chamber. The walls and floors were the same metal mesh that had made up the catwalk and other walkways spanning from platform to platform in the Engineer's lair. All around the room, except for this entrance and a matching exit on the opposite side, were more control panels like the ones they'd found in the last energy-core chamber.

"Now *this* is more like it." Emily grinned and released her sisters' hands to step across the metal-grated floor. "Three times the size of the energy-core chambers, at least. A heck of a lot shinier, too. Looks a lot more important, right?"

"Careful, Em." Laura slowly followed her sister into the chamber and tried to keep her eyes on everything at once. "We don't know what this place is for."

"But the lights turned on the minute we stepped inside and linked up."

Nickie trailed her hand along the mesh wall as she followed the huge curve of the room. "Linked up?"

"Yeah, you know. Holding hands. Supercharging our Hadstrom magic. Linking up."

"Or maybe this room was built for the original Hadstroms and not specifically for us."

"Laura." Emily turned around and stuck her hands on her hips. "I'm pretty sure that if this place was rigged to get rid of anyone who wasn't supposed to be here, it would've already noticed we *didn't* belong, and we'd be…I don't know. Not walking around in here like this."

"Maybe…"

Emily walked across the chamber toward one of the control panels. As soon as she touched it, the lights and buttons and small blank screens flared to life all around the room. She withdrew her hand and widened her eyes. "Woah."

"What did you do?"

"I turned it on. Relax." The youngest Hadstrom witch leaned forward for a closer look at all the little screens lining the control panels. "Hey, these kinda look like Grandma Eloise's old box TV, right? Kind gray-blue. A little grainy…"

"And they were made a heck of a long time before TVs were officially *invented.*" Laura's curiosity overcame her caution, and she went to join Emily by the lit-up screens. A low, steady hum rose from the old machinery of the ship. "This place definitely hasn't been used for a long time."

"But it all still works. I'm trying to figure out what's on these screens so we—wait a minute. Is that… *what?*"

Laura leaned closer to double-check, and her mouth fell open. "I don't believe it."

"Guys?" Nickie walked briskly across the large chamber, fighting back a small flutter of panic. "What's going on?"

"Okay, okay." Emily frantically waved her forward, then pointed at the closest screen on the far-right side of this section of control panels. "Nickie. Who does that look like to you?"

"A fuzzy outline of someone's head."

Laura pulled back. "No, you have to squint a little."

"Okay..." Nickie cocked her head, squinted, and almost jumped backward in surprise. "What the... Is that *Dad*?"

"Yeah, that's who it looks like."

"Hey, look." Emily pointed to the two other screens beside the one with Gregory Hadstrom's face frozen in grainy blue-gray. "That's Aunt Julie and Uncle Mark."

"No way."

"Totally." Emily's finger darted to another screen farther to the left. "And *that's* Grampy."

"That's not—" Laura leaned in again and blinked. "That *is* Grampy. He must be in his forties right there."

"Holy ancestors..." Emily breathed. "Literally. I bet you if we put these screens side by side with Grandma Eloise's old portrait room, all the faces would be the same."

"Not all the faces." Nickie scanned the screens and shook her head. "Grandma Eloise isn't in here. Or Mom. None of our family who married in on Dad's side, either."

Laura barked out a laugh and spread her arms, scanning the dozens of screens of the control panels. "These are all Hadstroms!"

"Woah..."

"The ship's been keeping tabs on the Hadstrom family for... I mean, it has to have been since the very first ones, right?" Laura tapped her finger against her lips a few times and stepped sideways along the panel to take in all the other faces. "Looks like they go back in time this way. Not like I remember all the faces in Grandma Eloise's portrait room, but the ones I recognize are moving right to left backward in time."

"Then the original Hadstrom witches would be all the way at the end." Nickie grinned. "We get to see their faces."

The two oldest Hadstrom sisters took off toward the far-left side of this specific section, scanning the faces in the tiny screens. "I wish there was some kind of labeling system."

"Yeah, it's pretty hard to tell which ones came first when they're all stacked on top of each other at the end."

Emily stayed where she was on the other side of the control panel, staring in disbelief at the image of their dad in the tiny screen. "This is so crazy..."

A tiny, round green light illuminated below the screen with Gregory Hadstrom's image and pulsed a few times. "Hey, what if all these screens are actually buttons?"

"Let's figure out what they're supposed to do before we—"

Laura's warning came too late. Emily pressed the screen with their dad's face, which depressed a little beneath her fingers with a soft, dusty click.

"Emily." Laura spread her arms at her youngest sister. "What are you doing? I said, let's figure out what they're supposed to do, first."

"That's what I just did." Emily scoffed and turned back toward the screen. "So now, let's see what it does."

The low hum filling the chamber grew in volume and pitch, then a large circle of blue light illuminated in the center of the floor. The Hadstrom sisters whirled around to face the center of the chamber, and a pale blue light filled that inner ring.

A projection of Gregory Hadstrom materialized in the center of the circle. He was at least twenty years younger, his hair quite a bit longer, and was furiously strumming on a guitar. The sound was slow to catch up, and it was filled with static when it wasn't sputtering off and on again. But the sound of their dad's playing was still unmistakable.

"Wow." Nickie grinned at the replayed image of their dad. "He really *was* good back in the day."

"This is a memory database." Laura shook her finger at Greg's projection and nodded. "Yeah, that's exactly what this is. All the information we need about the original Hadstroms—everything they did, probably even step by step—is right here in this room. If we find which one of these screens is them, we can literally playback whatever pieces of their memories this room stored up."

Emily slowly walked toward her sisters, her focus split between the young-looking Greg Hadstrom projection and her oldest sister spouting a bunch of stuff she didn't understand. "How do you know so much about a...what is it?"

"A memory database. Nathan and I talked about them a lot. That night he was helping me find the right combination of binding runes to put on the iron lance."

"Riveting conversation." Emily chuckled. "No wonder you guys fell asleep at the table."

"It was pretty cool. Between what few family stories he has and then what we found in that old journal of his uncle's, the Kashgar used to have memory banks like these everywhere. All over the ship."

"Keeping the family legacies alive, Kashgar-style." Nickie laughed and glanced at her thumb. "And we get rings."

"Well, we got *this* memory bank too, didn't we?" Laura gazed around the chamber and licked her lips. "I never thought I'd get to see something like this. I mean, the energy cores are one thing. And meeting a Velikan Engineer…"

"R.I.P., Rutilda." Emily put a fist to her heart, closed her eyes, and nodded.

"But to find *the* memory bank for Hadstrom witches? And wizards. This is incredible. We have the memories of every Hadstrom who's worn these rings and passed on the legacy to the next in line."

"Okay, then." Emily clapped her hands down on both of her sisters' shoulders and leaned forward over the control panels. "So, how do we figure out which of these are the original three?"

Laura and Nickie both set their hands on the control panel to lean forward and study the screen-faces more closely. The second their fingers touched the old metal, the projection of their dad cut off, and three screens on the far right lit up with those small, round green lights.

"That was ridiculously easy." Emily pointed toward the three pulsing lights. "How about all together, huh?"

"Worth a shot."

Together, the Hadstrom sisters reached out, and each

pushed one of the illuminated screens with who they hoped were the original Hadstroms—two wizards, one witch. The low hum rose again, only this time it went a lot higher in pitch before the blue circle in the center of the chamber flashed even brighter. The sisters turned around and got a full view of the original Hadstrom ancestors at the very beginning of their family legacy.

This was immediately clear because the first projection showed the original Hadstroms fighting off a Peabrain with glowing eyes coming after them. And even through the static and the audio that clicked on and off at irregular intervals, the Gorafrex's drumbeat came through with perfect clarity.

CHAPTER TWENTY-EIGHT

The Hadstrom sisters didn't have to do anything else with the control panels of the memory database in order to see everything they needed to know. The projections moved smoothly from one to the next, fading in and out with only a second or two in between. It showed their ancestors sitting down in a meeting with a group of Huldus, Kashgars, and *three* Velikan Engineers.

"That one's Rutilda." Emily pointed to the giant Velikan in the center. "It's the hair."

"Okay, be quiet, Em." Laura leaned back against the edge of the control panel and nearly held her breath. "It's hard enough to hear as it is."

They saw the meeting take place, heard most of the decision to build the prison out of the Isolation Vein of iron ore beneath the Greenbelt that would then become the center of the escape pod. They saw the original Hadstroms out in the thick woods beside Barton Creek, waving spells around with their wands to build a magical forge while one of the Velikan instructed them on the specifics of crafting their rings.

They saw the two Hadstrom brothers arguing over some part of the plan while their sister looked on in irritation. Eventually, she got their attention with a massively powerful shockwave of energy bursting right from the center of her ring.

The next projection showed the taller Hadstrom wizard with his version of the long iron lance Laura's legacy ring had built in the present. He practiced with it, training in the woods beside the prison while his sister used her version of the iron orbs like those Emily had used.

"What the heck is she doing with those?" Emily folded her arms and cocked her head. "I can't even follow it."

"Maybe making some kind of net?" Nickie shook her head. "I have no idea."

The second brother stood with his arms extended by his sides, eyes closed, singing a quiet but completely recognizable tune.

Nickie's eyes widened. "That's Dad's lullaby."

"If we didn't know where he got it before now…" Laura grinned. "What's that?"

Within the 3D projection, something crashed through the trees toward the original Hadstrom siblings. The magicals stepped toward each other, and all tipped something into their mouths at the same time. Then the sound cut out completely, and the Hadstrom ancestors turned to face the oncoming Gorafrex inside its human host from thousands of years ago. Trees crashed down around the enemy, cutting a wide path toward the witches it was so intent on devouring. Brilliant streams of blue-gray light shot from all three legacy rings and combined to form a massive, shimmering spell. The witches' mouths moved as one in some unheard chant, and then the projection cut out.

"Wait, what?" Laura stepped toward the ring of light in the center of the chamber, then spun around and pushed all three screens of the original Hadstroms one more time. The screens clicked, the hum rose in pitch, and the projection reappeared—back at the beginning of the sequence.

Nickie scratched the back of her head. "Looks like that's all we get."

"That can't be all we get." The next three times Laura pushed the screens, the projection cycled up again and played the memories from the beginning. "This was supposed to show us what we needed to know. How to fight the Gorafrex together and lock it up again."

"Let's give those big buttons a rest, though, okay?" Emily grabbed her big sister's wrists and gently pulled Laura way from the screens. "It's a lot easier to break something *this* old. Then you'd be really upset."

"Of course, I'm upset." Laura jerked her hands away and pulled absently on the bottom of her shirt. Then she smoothed it down again and drew a deep breath. "Because I really thought this was the end of us coming upon dead ends."

"Not a dead end, though." Nickie gestured toward the ring of blue light in the center of the chamber, which was now starting to fade. "We learned who the original Hadstroms were. We saw their faces. We saw how they made the rings and how closely they worked with the Huldus and Kashgars and Velikan."

"And we know that I've apparently been using those

iron orbs wrong this whole time." Emily snorted. "Plus, the fact that there's a potion and chanting involved. I wish the sound hadn't cut out at that point, though."

"Potion?" Laura frowned.

"Yeah. You know..." Emily mimed knocking back a drink of one kind or another. "They each threw back a potion right before they went all Hadstrom magic on that approaching Gorafrex. Which, by the way, seemed a lot more powerful back then than it does now. I mean, it hasn't cut down dozens of trees since we've been fighting it."

"Yeah, but that Peabrain it was using was awakened *before* the Gorafrex took it as a host." Nickie scanned the faces of all their Hadstrom-legacy ancestors one more time. "Way back then, right after this ship left Arenya V, all the Peabrains were awakened and could use their magic, remember. That one had already stepped into its full power before it became a host. And I bet that made it a lot more dangerous, whoever it was."

"That still doesn't help *us* figure out what to do next." Laura sighed and shook her head. "So, now what? We're back at square one. Honestly, I'm ready to pull out Tiberius' potions and get out of here before we run out of time. And who knows how long we have until the Gorafrex figures out—"

"Check *that* out." Grinning, Emily pointed across the chamber toward the opposite entrance. The blue and green scrolling lights had started back up again, illuminating the passage on the other side every few seconds before they disappeared into the darkness and started all over again. "Laura, you're in luck. This is definitely not the end."

"Huh." The oldest Hadstrom sister cleared her throat and adopted a re-determined smile. "That might be the best thing you've said all night, Em."

"Oh, great. Thanks. Let's hope I can come up with something better than *that*."

Nickie chuckled, caught Emily's gaze, and nodded toward Laura, who'd already taken off across the chamber toward the opposite entrance. "Looks like we have a lot more walking to do. Try to keep up, huh?"

Emily shot her sister a frown of mock seriousness and nodded vigorously. "Yes, yes. Of course. I wouldn't want to fall behind while we're on such an important mission."

As soon as the Hadstrom witches stepped out of the chamber and into the next blue-and-green-lit passage beyond, the lights behind them blinked out completely with another loud, echoing click.

"I know it's silly, guys, but I can't help but think that giant bang sounds like somebody sliding a deadbolt behind us."

"We have the Huldu's potion, Em. That'll get us out if we really need to use it." Laura's voice moved quickly down the passage before her silhouette was briefly illuminated by the flashing lights lighting the passage floor one more time. "But I'm sure it's not nearly as awesome as anything you've whipped up for us before."

"Hey." Emily grinned and walked with a little more bounce in her step. "That was a super nice thing to say, Laura. I'm honored. Really."

"Well, I'm feeling a little more optimistic. We'll see what happens when we get to the end of *this* tunnel."

Nickie reached back and patted the teardrop-shaped

potion vial from Tiberius, to make sure it was still safe and ready to use if they needed it.

CHAPTER TWENTY-NINE

They didn't come to the end of the tunnel for a long, long time.

"I would *really* like to know what time it is right now." Emily drew her fingertips along both sides of the tunnel, which were smooth and hardly crumbled at all beneath her touch. "Because it feels like we've been walking slightly uphill for *hours*. And I'm not even tired."

"It does beg the question, doesn't it?" Laura kept trudging along the corridor, her pace unbroken and as steady as when they'd set out.

Nickie waited a few extra seconds, then added, "What question?"

"How long we've been walking."

"Right. I'm with Em, though. I'm not even a little tired, either."

Laura let out a thoughtful hum. "Probably the excitement of walking through a mysteriously dark tunnel, following a bunch of flashing lights, with no idea where we're headed after we watched the actual memories of our ancestors starting this whole Hadstrom legacy in the first place."

The tunnel fell silent for a few seconds, then Emily pointed up ahead at Laura, although nobody could see her. She could barely see her finger. "*Or* we could be walking up this giant tunnel forever. Maybe it's endless. Maybe we're in a dream."

"That all three of us are having at the same time? Come on, Em."

"Maybe that metal staircase led us down into a different dimension like the Clubhouse, only instead of being boxed off by space, this one goes on forever *without time...*"

Nickie burst out laughing. "Where did you come up with this stuff, Em?"

"Just my thoughts. I've had all this time of walking without any change of scenery. It's scary in my head, Nickie. You don't even know."

"Yeah, I think I have a pretty good idea."

"Do you guys see that?" Without thinking or warning anyone, Laura stopped in the passageway before the next round of flashing lights blinked from behind and passed ahead of them. Nickie bumped into her sister's back and was instantly sandwiched between Laura and Emily.

The youngest Hadstrom sister grunted and reared back, clutching her nose. "A little warning would've been nice."

"Sorry." Laura was too distracted by what she'd seen to try making it sound any more genuine. "Look up ahead for a minute. Do you see that?"

"Hmm...darkness, darkness, and more—oh. Wait."

Emily squinted, grabbed Nickie's shoulders, and leaned forward to peer around her sister. "That kinda looks like a light."

"Exactly. And not a blue or green flashing light, either." Laura nodded, her determination that much more restored. "So, let's go figure out where we've been heading this whole time."

Nickie slowly stepped out of Emily's hold and kept walking. "Looks like your theory about being stuck in a timeless tunnel to nowhere just got debunked, Em."

"Oh, I wasn't super attached to it. Don't worry. I have plenty more theories where that came from." She tapped her temple, but of course, nobody could see that, either.

They followed the light for another indeterminable length of time, and the only indication that they were getting closer came from the slowly growing light at the end of the tunnel and the fact that the incline had risen sharply.

"Whew." Emily huffed along at the end of the line, helping to push herself up after her sisters by shoving both hands against the walls of the tunnel. "This turned into a serious hike. Underground."

"This is what I'm guessing Laura does a lot more of when it comes to exploring pits and walking through tunnels."

"Sort of." Laura's breathing had grown a little heavier, too, but she still hadn't slowed down. "The main difference now is that when I'm out in the field, I have an idea of where I am, where I'm going, and what I'm looking for. Then I find it. So, this still isn't nearly as satisfying."

"But we're working up a good sweat!" Emily stuck her tongue out, gave herself two seconds to rest, then pushed forward again. After a few more yards, she almost fell forward on her face when the passage walls she'd been using as leverage didn't exist the next time she tried to push against them. She stumbled forward with a yelp of surprise, then the blue and green lights flashed by beneath the missing pieces of the tunnel wall. It gave her a brief glimpse of jagged stone and black, gaping holes on either side of her. "Hey, be careful up here, guys."

"What's up?"

"We walked past two huge holes in the tunnel walls. Almost like something smashed right through them. So, you know, be careful. Things might be a little shaky."

"Thanks for the warning, Em." Laura didn't slow at all. "I think we're almost there."

The warm, pale-yellow glow was growing brighter and larger ahead of them. Now that they could gauge the distance with that light, it only took the sisters a few more minutes before they'd climbed up the rest of the tunnel, which curved a little at the end and stopped.

"It's a door," Laura said flatly.

"What?" Emily wiped a thin layer of sweat from her forehead and joined her sisters at the top. "Aw, man. I thought for sure we were finally making it out of the tunnels altogether. We could've been walking for so long that we went all the way through the night and into morning. Maybe."

"Maybe, but that's not what this is." Laura folded her arms, then lifted one hand again to tap two fingers against her lips. "It's definitely a door. Or two."

"Like elevator doors, maybe?" Nickie pointed to the thin seam in the center, which was the only part of the entire rectangle that wasn't glowing with the soft yellow light.

"Ha. That'd be pretty freakin' ironic." Emily huffed out a laugh and snorted a few times, then bent over with her hands on her knees to catch her breath. "We hiked up this way to get to an elevator."

"It's not an elevator. But it opens. Somehow." Laura spread her hands in front of the door, searching for markings or directional symbols. Nothing. So, she pressed both hands against the doors. The yellow glow flashed weakly, but that was it.

"Yeah, maybe it's like the screen buttons and pretty much everything else we've touched lately." Emily stepped up beside her sisters and held her palms toward the door. "On three."

"One...two...three."

The Hadstrom witches pressed their hands against the glowing golden doors at the same time. The light responded with a much stronger pulse, then the stone doors beneath their palms shuddered, groaned, and finally slid apart from the center before retracting into the rest of the stone walls at the end of the tunnel.

"But pretty much like an elevator door," Nickie repeated with a smirk.

When they stepped through, Nickie and Emily both experienced the same strong waves of déjà vu.

"Wait a minute..." Emily pointed at the large silver streak running through the floor right ahead of them and then the door on the opposite side of the small chamber. "We've been here before."

"Yeah." Nickie blinked with wide eyes at the tiny, sealed chamber lit by the same soft yellow glow as the door they'd opened. "That means we walked all the way from Rutilda's lair under the history museum to the middle of the Barton Creek Greenbelt. Underground."

Laura scoffed. "There's no way we're at the Greenbelt."

"Laura." Nickie turned to catch her sister's gaze and put a hand on Laura's shoulder. "That's the Isolation Vein."

"The—" Laura's smile vanished, and she turned quickly toward the streak of glistening iron running across the stone floor. "No..."

"Oh, yeah." Emily pointed at a divot in the smooth iron vein. "See that? That's where Nickie sang a chunk of pure iron out of the ground and pulled it out."

"So, we're..." Laura rubbed her cheeks a few times and cocked her head. "We're standing right next to the Gorafrex's prison."

"Pretty much." Nickie leaned forward and peered at the door to the Isolation Vein, which she and Emily had helped Nathan open by powering his Kashgar magic. "But I don't know how we're standing in this room right now. The whole watchtower was destroyed. The Greenbelt flooded, the Tree Folk saved us... All that actually happened."

"Maybe your theory about time moving in a different direction isn't all that far off the mark, Em."

"Except we didn't go back in time..." Emily shot her sisters an apologetic glance and shrugged. "At least now I know where those holes in the tunnel walls came from."

Laura frowned, and Emily and Nickie said at the same time, "The dwarven hammer."

The oldest Hadstrom sister's mouth fell open, and it took her a few seconds to think of anything at all. "Then this room somehow wasn't destroyed."

"I guess. How?" Emily shrugged. "Beats me completely."

On their right, another soft glow illuminated in what had previously looked like more rock wall in the chamber holding the Isolation Vein. When the shape of another set of doors made itself perfectly clear, the witches hesitantly crossed the small chamber, being careful not to step directly on the iron vein. This second set of doors opened on its own before they had a chance to open it with their touch.

The doors finished sliding back into place within the stone walls, and the Hadstrom sisters were assaulted by a gust of frigid air that smelled like dust and old pennies. The silence greeting them on the other side of this new set of doors was absolute and deafening.

"You know, I don't think that's something we need to go explore." Emily lifted a finger and found herself unable to stare directly into the darkness. "Whatever that is, it's giving me a super bad feeling."

Behind the sisters, thin, snaking tendrils poked through the earth and breached the ceiling of the Isolation Vein's chamber, moving slowly and silently enough that none of the witches noticed.

"I'm right there with you, Em." Nickie reached out and grabbed her little sister's hand. "I was willing to trust the unfolding metal staircase and the flashing lights. That memory database was cool, too. But this? This isn't meant for us. Right?"

They both turned to look at Laura, who now clenched her eyes so tightly shut that it looked like she was in pain.

"Laura?" Nickie reached out to softly lay a hand on her big sister's back. "You okay?"

"Yeah, I'm just… I'm trying to remember what he said."

The tree roots dropped farther into the open chamber behind the Hadstrom sisters, dangling and moving stealthily forward.

"What who said?"

"Something about…binding the past to the future. Or maybe the healing to the wound…"

"She's talking about Astro, Em."

"Laura, did he tell you about *this*? Or why we were led all the way up here?"

"No, it's a…something about…" Laura pressed a hand to her temple and pushed herself to focus even harder.

The tree roots dropped the last few feet behind the Hadstrom sisters, and a few pebbles dropped from the earthen ceiling before clattering across the stone floor. Nickie and Emily both turned around to see an entire network of roots reaching toward them like creepy fingers.

"Laura!"

"That's it!" Laura's eyes shot open, and she grinned into the cold darkness in front of them. "The heart beneath the earth binds the blood to itself!"

All the tree roots instantly flared with the same bright-blue glow that had rescued the witches from the final exploding energy core.

"But that would mean—"

Laura never got to finish her thought. The glowing roots lashed out like striking snakes and pushed all three Hadstrom sisters over the ledge and into the cold, silent, empty darkness of the Gorafrex's iron prison. As the witches' shouts of surprise fell through the nothingness and faded away, the glowing golden doors closed on their own with a long echo of finality.

CHAPTER THIRTY

"Laura!" Emily thought she moved through the darkness, but she couldn't be sure. There was no bottom beneath her feet, no light or sound but her voice, and the feeling of falling through all that nothingness had only lasted a few seconds before the doors banged shut and everything else ceased to exist.

"Nickie? Can you guys hear me?"

From somewhere very far away, she thought she heard her name.

"Laura?"

"Em!" The voice was closer this time, and it had a strangely disjointed echo.

"Nickie!"

"I can't see anything. Where are you?"

"Wait, what's that? I see a light."

"Yeah, I see it too. It's right in front of me."

"And it's—" Emily stopped and thought she was staring at a glowing green reflection of herself for a few seconds until she realized she was staring at Nickie's face in the darkness. "Hey!"

"Oh, thank the ancestors." Laura's face illuminated next in the rising green light growing between the sisters. "You guys okay?"

"Uh…yeah." Emily glanced down—at least, she thought it was down—but couldn't see anything else. "Are we floating?"

"Flying, suspended, falling. I don't know, Em."

"What about that?" Nickie's arm appeared from the darkness so she could point at the growing sphere of green light in the middle of the circle the three witches now formed.

"No idea." Laura tried to laugh, but it came out as more of a weak grunt. "Guess we don't really have any other choice, right? Just watch, I guess."

And they did. The Hadstrom sisters floated or flew or fell through the nothingness of the Gorafrex's eternal prison and stared into the green glow. Then the visions started.

The light jerked them through star systems and galaxies, farther across the universe than anyone now living on this ship could imagine. When the movement slowed, the sisters were looking at a planet with three moons—a planet that sustained life and magic and more races than those living together on the ship called Earth.

That's Arenya V. Emily thought she'd said it out loud, but she couldn't hear her voice anymore.

The visions flashed quickly after that, one right after the other. Witches and wizards living peacefully on their homeworld, casting spells and crafting magic and advancing their knowledge in harmony with the other races. Multiple masses of shimmering, ethereal forms floating through forests, across meadows, over oceans. A single energetic being stopping in front of a powerful awakened Peabrain on Arenya V.

The two beings seemed to study each other—one Peabrain and one Gorafrex in its true, incorporeal form. The Peabrain reached out, and the Gorafrex retracted only a little in hesitation. Then the shimmering mass extended a piece of itself toward the Peabrain, and they joined.

More images flashed again. Gorafrex and Peabrain working together to cast powerful magic. Helping other magicals of Arenya V to build civilizations, advance magical technology. Two more Peabrains joined with Gorafrex beings. The numbers of these partnerships grew, and Arenya V flourished.

Emily blinked—or thought she did. *That's not what we've been told about the Gorafrex.*

The planet moved through seasons and cycles until the visions stopped again at the original Peabrain host to what she assumed was the same Gorafrex being. The Peabrain's eyes lit up with a shimmering glow as he spoke to a middle-aged wizard. They had no voices—no sound existed in this space without space in which the Hadstrom sisters now existed—but the wizard was clearly angry. The Peabrain looked a little frustrated, but more than anything, he looked terribly sad.

Why does that wizard look so familiar?

Emily had the memory just at the back of her head, but before she could grasp it, the wizard in the vision took out his wand and pointed it at the Peabrain-Gorafrex. Magic flew in all directions. The magicals fought each other, and thick, smoky darkness descended upon the wizard. His eyes glowed too, now, but it wasn't with the Gorafrex's light or the Peabrain's hope.

If this were in color, that wizard's eyes would be black.

The rest of the soundless story burst through Emily's head so quickly, she thought she was screaming by the end of it. So much destruction. So much pain and fear and death. Thriving civilizations fell beneath dark magic. And in an instant, all the Gorafrex turned. They took Peabrain hosts against their will. Hunted witches and wizards to take what they wanted from blood magic. Killed the same magicals they'd been helping for centuries.

The visions ended with a much smaller planet moving slowly away from Arenya V.

Not a planet... Emily's head was pounding, but she couldn't look away from the vision, even when she thought she'd clenched her eyes shut. *That's Earth. That's the ship.*

A single weak, desperate light pierced the atmosphere of Arenya V and disappeared inside the much smaller shape of the ship called Earth before that ship launched itself on its maiden voyage, never to reach its destination.

The green light of the visions within the Gorafrex prison burst in every direction, blinding the Hadstrom sisters to everything. And then the nothingness returned.

Emily tried to call out to her sisters again and got no response—because her voice never made it past her lips. There was nothing left.

CHAPTER THIRTY-ONE

The next thing Laura felt after so much nothingness was icy-cold wetness around her knees and hands. She gasped when she felt it and heard something splashing on either side of her. Water trickled gently, coming from every direction, and the drone of cicadas and crickets cut through the silence she'd thought would never end.

"Oh, man..." Emily took a gasping breath and lurched forward again on her hands and knees. Then she pushed herself up, sat back on her heels, and turned to look at Laura. "Did you see that?"

On the other side of Laura, Nickie scooped up a handful of water and splashed it over her face. "That was real."

Laura swallowed. "That was so real. So is this."

She finally let herself look up from the dark wetness beneath her and already knew where they were before she saw it. So many dogwood trees and live oaks lined the banks of Barton Creek, but right above the Hadstrom sisters—over the center of the creek itself—the night sky was studded with billions of glittering stars. And upriver a few yards in front of them was the single willow growing from the berm in the center of the creek.

"Nice trick with the tree roots," she muttered. "Pushing us into the actual prison."

"And spitting us right back out again." Emily drew another few deep breaths, then tried to stand. Her knees buckled, but she caught herself on the slippery stones of the riverbed with a smaller splash. "I'm soaked."

"I know, Em. Let's get out of the creek, at least." Laura turned toward Nickie and reached out her hand. "You okay?"

"Yeah." Nickie nodded, her long, soaked hair sticking to her neck and face and dropping over her shoulders when she bent her head. "Yeah, I'm okay. That was…"

"I know. Come on."

The Hadstrom sisters dragged themselves carefully across the slick, algae-covered rocks. The stars and the half-moon gave them more than enough light to see by, but it was still a slow process. Emily reached the bank first, sat down on the pebbly beach, and reached out to help first Laura and then Nickie crawl out of the creek. Laura sat next to her youngest sister, and Nickie crawled a little farther away from the water before leaning sideways and rolling from her hands and knees onto her back. Her arms crunched down into the tiny pebbles, and she closed her eyes.

"That was the craziest thing I've ever been through."

"You can say that again."

The sisters fell silent for a few seconds until Nickie said again, "That was the craziest thing I've ever been through."

Laura burst out laughing, and Emily wasn't too far behind her. Nickie opened her eyes to stare at the stars and found herself chuckling with her sisters until her ribs gave her grief again and she forced herself to stop.

"I gotta give it to you, Em. Your theories on our hike up that tunnel were a lot closer than we gave you credit for."

"You mean like how we went through space and time without space and time?"

Laura chuckled and pulled her wet hair back away from her face. "And the whole part about the three of us sharing the same dream. Couldn't wrap my head around that until a few minutes ago."

"Oh, yeah. I did say that, didn't I?"

They sat in silence for a few more minutes, quickly warming up in the nighttime heat after the frigid darkness of the prison and then the shockingly cool water of the creek. Emily drew a deep breath and looked up at the moonlit sky again. "Everything we thought we knew about the Gorafrex is wrong, isn't it?"

"Maybe not everything." Nickie grabbed a handful of pebbles and let them sift through her fingers. "The Gorafrex still needs a human host to do anything, so that hasn't changed."

"But you guys saw that first one, right? The Peabrain actually *wanted* the Gorafrex to...join with it." Emily shook her head. "My mind is totally blown right now."

"And what about that wizard?" Nickie added. "The man...I mean, he went dark."

"All the way dark." Emily dropped her head and leaned over her crossed legs. "Dark magic wizard fighting with a Peabrain-Gorafrex super-team."

"That's what went wrong." Laura tapped her fingers against her lips and nodded. "That's exactly what went wrong. Not the Gorafrex beings as a race hunting and killing witches and wizards. Not this one Gorafrex sneaking onto the ship before it left Arenya V. Not even me letting it out of the prison again."

She nodded toward the willow, so many long, thin branches like a thick curtain rustling in the breeze. "It was the wizard. Something happened, and that wizard turned dark."

"You think that's what turned the Gorafrex against our race?"

"Yeah, Em. That's exactly what I think happened. I'm not sure what it was or how, but that doesn't really matter at this point."

"That wizard..." Emily frowned and shut her eyes to try pulling the face up from her memory. "Oh! I knew there was something familiar about him."

Nickie slowly pushed her back off the beach and propped herself up on her forearms. "So did I. Couldn't place it, though. That was so long ago, there's no way we've seen him before."

"No, but we see pieces of him every day, don't we?" Emily turned halfway around on the pebbly beach to shoot Nickie a wide-eyed stare of comprehension. "In the mirror."

"Oh, man..." Nickie swallowed and looked at Laura, just to double-check. "That wizard who turned dark?"

"A Hadstrom wizard going even farther back than the original three on this ship. Yeah." Laura glanced down at her silver legacy ring glistening in the moonlight. "Those three were only the beginning on this ship. And none of the histories go back any farther than that because we don't have access to anything before this ship set out. That's all still back on Arenya V, wherever it is. That's why we haven't been able to figure any of this out."

"Our bloodline and our legacy to protect this ship from the Gorafrex started with a wizard who went dark and used that darkness to destroy half of our homeworld." Nickie shook her head in amazement. "What does that say about us, huh?"

"Hey, don't start going down that road, Nickie. Got it?" Laura pointed at her sister. "We're not that dark wizard, whether or not he was an actual Hadstrom or merely started the whole thing. But we are *not* like him."

"That never crossed *my* mind." Emily turned to crawl on her hands and knees toward Nickie. Then she sat up and wrapped her big sister in a hug. "So, you need to shut that thinking down right now. Do not pass Go. Do not collect two hundred dollars. For real, Nickie."

"Sure, yeah. Sorry."

"Don't be." Laura tried to stand, gave up, and opted for crawling up the beach like Emily to sit on the other side of the middle Hadstrom sister. "This has been a weird day."

They all offered up weak chuckles at that.

Laura wrapped her arms around Nickie's shoulders too, covering Emily's arms with hers. "We're not anything like that first dark wizard. That's for sure. But that's where we came from. And we still have the memory of what he was and what he did living inside us."

"Uh…" Emily let out a dry, disbelieving laugh. "I'm not sure I can even pretend to know what you mean by that."

"I mean, we're the only ones who can do what needs to be done with the Gorafrex." Laura gave Nickie's shoulders and Emily's arms a little squeeze. "And it's not what we thought it was."

Nickie lifted her head and met her big sister's gaze. "We don't have to use a bunch of potions and weird iron weapons to lock it up in the prison again?"

"Nope." The oldest Hadstrom witch offered both her sisters a reassuring smile, although she knew how they'd react to what she was about to say. "We don't have to lock it up at all. We need to free it."

"Huh. I think you lost most of your brain cells to that vision, Laura."

"Em, I'm serious. The whole witch-killing part of the Gorafrex…that's not what that creature was made to do. That's not its true nature, right? Something happened with that first wizard who went dark, and because we're the descendants of that bloodline, we're the only ones who can fix it."

"So, you're saying forgive and forget because it's not that thing's *fault* that it kills witches and wizards for blood magic?"

"No. I'm saying we figure out what needs to be done to reverse what happened on Arenya V way back before the ship was even built. And then we do *that*."

Nickie sniffed and stared out across the moonlight glistening on the water of Barton Creek. "How are we gonna figure that out? No one else knows about this. And no one's gonna believe us now."

"Well, I guess we start with picking apart what Astro told me in his weird little scrying riddle." Laura grinned.

"Because I remember all of it now, and it's starting to make sense."

"Okay." Nickie nodded. "We'll start with that, then."

The sisters sat in silence for a few more minutes, each of them going over the visions from the Gorafrex prison over and over in their minds. Emily drew a sharp breath and shot her sisters a crooked grin. "Hey, so when we were in there, there was this point where I could see you guys *and* the vision, but I couldn't hear anything. Or say anything. But we were all there."

"Where are you going with this?" Nickie wrinkled her nose.

"What if…okay, hear me out. What if the three of us were *inside* each other's *heads* for that whole funky vision thing?"

Laura blew a raspberry and shook her head. "No way. Maybe hundreds of thousands of years ago on Arenya V, but I don't think anyone on this ship can read minds anymore. If they ever did in the first place."

"Hey, you guys said my theories about timeless tunnels and sharing the same dream were a total joke." Emily withdrew her arms from around Nickie and folded them instead. "Until they weren't."

"Okay, how about this." Nickie pressed her lips together and tried not to laugh. "We won't write off the whole mind-reading thing until we have total and complete proof that it's possible. But I'm not saying it's possible until it happens, okay?"

"Yeah. Deal." Emily stuck out her hand, Nickie shook it firmly, and Laura laughed.

"Come on. Let's go home. I don't know what time it is,

but I bet Chuck and Nathan are passed out somewhere in our house, hoping we didn't fall into a bottomless pit or something."

Emily laughed. "Boy, are *they* gonna be disappointed."

The Hadstrom sisters are busy deciphering the prophecy. It ends up with them having a LONG to-do list and not a lot of time to get it done. Can the sisters pull together all the parts needed from the past and present to reverse all the darkness brought by a dark wizard long ago? Find out in *Magic Unbound*.

Get sneak peeks, exclusive giveaways, behind the scenes content, and more.
PLUS you'll be notified of special **one day only fan pricing** on new releases.

Sign up today to get free stories.

CLICK HERE

or visit: https://marthacarr.com/read-free-stories/

AUTHOR NOTES - MARTHA CARR

APRIL 6, 2020

Interesting tidbits from inside the quarantine.

1. A donut shop posted in my neighborhood's Facebook group that he would have hot, fresh donuts and coffee for sale Saturday morning. Just come park in the lot by the amenity center by 9:45 am and they would sell them by the box – no special orders. You pull up, you get a box for $12. Sounds simple, right?

It would have been, except the donut shop brought 30 boxes and about a hundred cars showed up. We may all be going a little stir crazy and need a sugar fix. Is that a bad sign?

He hurriedly called for more and he's coming back next weekend, better prepared. I heard there were even a few heated arguments from at least six feet away.

Several entrepreneurial neighbors filled in the void by advertising cheesecake, blueberry muffins, cakes and cookies for sale. There were a lot of takers. We are going to roll out of this quarantine licking our fingers and blinking at the light.

2. My Facebook feed is now filled with pictures of women showing off their gray roots and at least one friend has asked how to get off gel nail polish (100% acetone that's in any grocery store or Target). Things are getting very real. I keep making a hair appointment for the next month and then moving it when necessary. Eventually, I'll have it right and it will be the most satisfying haircut I've ever gotten.

3. Reading Guardians of Magic from the Leira Chronicles during Adult Story Time every weekday at one pm CT is going well. More and more people are tuning in and yes, on Friday I forgot to turn on the lights. It looked like I was reading from the shadows, somewhere deep in quarantine protection. Come listen if you need a distraction – and every day's reading is on my YouTube channel so you can binge and catch up. You can watch my hair getting longer over time like a live chia pet.

4. I saw a neighbor running down the street today carrying a large, human body-sized duffel bag over his shoulder. Exercise? Solution for that nagging spouse during quarantine? Hard to say. I had to keep at least six feet away.

5. Michael Anderle and I have taken to making jokes with hashtags in a long string of words like when he was on a plane coming home and I sent him a string of #youcanhavethearmrest, #smellsliketroubleinhere, #canIputmyselfintheoverhead. You get the idea. We have kept this up, even in other people's channels confusing everyone but ourselves. That may not be from the quarantine. That may just be our usual selves.

6. Every day I like to remind myself of all the small

apartments I've lived in and could have been quarantined in – and feel the gratitude wash over me one more time that I am in my dream house the troll built.

Take good care of yourselves people and find a little joy in every day. More adventures to follow.

OTHER BOOKS BY MARTHA CARR

(AND THERE'S A LOT OF THEM)

Other series in the Terranavis Universe:

The Adventures of Maggie Parker
The Adventures of Finnegan Dragonbender

If you enjoyed this series, you may enjoy these series in the Oriceran Universe:

THE LEIRA CHRONICLES
I FEAR NO EVIL
REWRITING JUSTICE
SCHOOL OF NECESSARY MAGIC
SCHOOL OF NECESSARY MAGIC: RAINE CAMPBELL
ALISON BROWNSTONE
THE DANIEL CODEX SERIES
FEDERAL AGENTS OF MAGIC
SCIONS OF MAGIC
THE UNBELIEVABLE MR. BROWNSTONE
THE KACY CHRONICLES

MIDWEST MAGIC CHRONICLES
SOUL STONE MAGE
THE FAIRHAVEN CHRONICLES

OTHER BOOKS BY JUDITH BERENS

OTHER BOOKS BY MARTHA CARR

OTHER BOOKS BY MICHAEL ANDERLE

JOIN THE TERRANAVIS UNIVERSE FAN GROUP ON FACEBOOK!

BOOKS BY MICHAEL ANDERLE

For a complete list of books by Michael Anderle, please visit

www.lmbpn.com/ma-books/

All LMBPN Audiobooks are Available at Audible.com and iTunes. For a complete list of audiobooks visit:

www.lmbpn.com/audible

CONNECT WITH THE AUTHORS

Martha Carr Social

Website:
http://www.marthacarr.com

Facebook:
https://www.facebook.com/groups/MarthaCarrFans/

https://www.facebook.com/terranavisuniverse/

Michael Anderle Social

Michael Anderle Social
Website:
http://www.lmbpn.com

Email List:
http://lmbpn.com/email/

Facebook
https://www.facebook.com/TheKurtherianGambitBooks/

www.ingramcontent.com/pod-product-compliance
Lightning Source LLC
Chambersburg PA
CBHW031649100726
47898CB00006B/2030